remember that night

KATRINA MARIE

Follow your dreams, and your heart.
You never know where they may lead you.

THE MIRROR in the bathroom is foggy from the shower. The towel leaving streaks across the glass as I wipe it to see my reflection. Blonde hair in stringy wet tendrils, eyes wide with nerves and excitement.

The Fall semester starts in a week, and this is the last time I will be able to see *him*. I wasn't looking for a relationship over the summer. But he charmed me and made me laugh. I thought it was going to be just a fling. One last hoorah before I started over in a new town. Not that I had any sort of relationship prior to him. Nobody goes for the geeky, quiet girl.

I blow dry my hair, trying to decide what I'm going to wear tonight. A pink sundress hangs over my door, but I don't think I want to wear it anymore. I want tonight to be special...for both of us.

As soon as I shut the blow dryer off, I walk into my

room and head straight for the walk-in closet. It's not huge, but it's a decent size. I don't have enough clothes to fill it. On the right side, my fandom t-shirts hang in all their glory. Everything from *Harry Potter* to *The Walking Dead*. Jeans line the shelves below them. On the left, and the emptiest area of my closet, hang the very few dresses I own. Aside from the dress hanging on my bathroom door.

I slide the hangers to the side, searching for the perfect dress. Too plain. Too blah. Pushing over three more dresses, I find the perfect one. It's the one thing all girls have in their closets. The little black dress. The last time I wore mine was during my induction into the honor society.

The floor is littered with sneakers, Vans, and Converse. I know there are a few pairs of heels in here somewhere. I shuffle through the shoes, throwing them aside. It looks like a minefield in here. Finally, I find the black heels I'm looking for. Inspecting them, I'm not that crazy about wearing them. But, they are the only pair I have so they will have to work.

Shoes in one hand, I use the other to pull the dress off the hanger and place them on my bed. My curling iron is plugged in and heating up. I open my makeup case and study the few contents in there. Mascara, lip gloss, and eyeshadows in neutral colors.

I don't bother with the eyeshadow or lip gloss. Instead I sweep the mascara onto my lashes, then go to

Mom's bathroom. She has so much makeup. I don't even know what half of it is, but I spot a tube of lipstick and grab it before heading back to my room.

The curling iron slides to the bottom of my hair easily. Forming small waves at the ends, just enough to give my hair a little bit of bounce. I open the tube of lipstick. It's bright red. I've never worn this color before, and I'm not sure I can pull it off, but I put it on anyway.

The girl looking back at me in the mirror is not the one I was before getting ready. The bright lipstick makes me feel more mature and confident. Like I can conquer the world.

Rushing down the hall, I call out, "Mom, Dad. I'm going out, I'll be back later."

"Okay, honey," Mom says from the kitchen. "Be careful."

"I will." That's the thing about being the good, nerdy girl. Your parents don't even bother asking where you're going. They just assume it's to meet up with friends from various school clubs. I've never even had a curfew.

Grabbing my keys, I walk out the door, and practically sprint to my car. Ready to see the guy that's stolen my heart.

* * *

It's ten 'til seven when I pull up to the restaurant. This place is packed. How are we even going to get a seat?

After parking the car, I take one last look in the visor mirror, making sure my lipstick hasn't smudged. There's a bench right outside the restaurant and I take a seat to wait.

Twenty minutes later I still haven't gotten a response. Maybe he's stuck in traffic or can't find his keys. I text him, hoping he'll answer.

Darcy: Are you almost here?

Another ten minutes go by, then thirty, and still no response. Tears are welling up in my eyes, but I refuse to let them fall. I can't believe he stood me up. He's always been early. I don't understand. Was he just playing me?

Barely containing my sadness, I march to my car, unlock the door, and slide into my seat. The second the door is closed, I let my sobs free. Let all the emotion welling up inside me find their way out through the hot, salty tears streaming down my face.

Another half hour has passed before the tears begin to slow, and anger takes control. I was so stupid to think someone like him would ever want someone like me. He's attractive, athletic, and the complete opposite of who I am. The shy, meek girl. The one nobody truly sees.

With a new resolve, I put the key in the ignition and start my car. I leave for Hilltown University next weekend. It's time for a change. I will not be the girl everyone sees through. Don't get me wrong, I'm not going to be a party animal either. But, it's time for my nerdy ways to hit the road.

Never again will I let someone make me feel the way I feel tonight. He may have broken my naïve heart by not showing up, but he is also the catalyst to a new and improved version of me.

darcy

"JANE," I call out, placing the steaming hot cup of coffee on the counter. An older woman approaches the counter, hand already outstretched for the drink that will give her the fuel she needs to conquer the day. "Here's your soy latte. Come back and see us."

The cup is already to her lips before she turns around, hand in the air giving an awkward backwards wave. I'll see her bright and early in the morning. This is her first stop before heading to her corporate job. Roasted is one of the few small coffee shops around, and we take pride in knowing what our customers want.

"Do we need any more muffins up there?" Cami hollers from the back. I will never understand why she can't walk up here to ask me if we need anything, but I love her just the same.

The door swishes softly as I push it open. "No, we're good."

"Dude, you didn't have to walk back here to tell me that."

"I know, but I don't really want to yell in front of the customers," I sigh.

She spins around, placing a pan full of muffin batter into the oven. I can almost feel the eye roll that is no doubt directed toward me.

"What time is it?" She asks. "We *do* have classes we have to attend today."

"Don't remind me," I mutter. Last year, I didn't feel the dread that I feel now. The first day of classes has always been my favorite thing. Though, I won't admit that out loud. But this year, that just ups the chances that I will run into *him*.

It seems Derrick's little trip to visit Travis last semester made him decide that he wanted to attend Hilltown University. It would be my luck the one guy that shattered my heart would be the best friend of my best friend's boyfriend. Talk about a small freaking world.

"Darcy," Cami snaps her fingers in front of my face. "The time?"

"Oh, sorry," I say. "We need to leave in fifteen minutes if we want to get cleaned up."

"Damn straight I want to at least shower. As much as I love coffee, there's no way in hell I want to walk into class smelling like I swam in it."

I peek through the door to see if there are any customers. There's a man, late fifties, with his eyebrows furrowed. Of course, there would be someone to hear

Cami's loud exclamations. We need to work on inside voices, even when she's working in the kitchen.

Stepping back behind the counter, I place a too wide smile on my face. "What can I get you this morning, sir?"

"Just a coffee."

"Would you like anything added to it?"

"No," he grumbles. "I like it just the way it comes out of the machine."

Who pissed in his cereal this morning? He could have just as easily made his own coffee at home. But I don't let my frustration with his attitude show. "Coming right up."

The rest of my shift goes by quickly. Most of the people coming in are regulars and I know their orders like the back of my hand. Cami places fresh muffins in the display case, and before I have a chance to grab one, she whisks me from behind the counter and toward the front door.

"What about my bag?"

"I have it right here," she lifts up the bag in question. "And, I already clocked us out."

I regret the day I gave her the code to clock me in. "Um, okay."

"I can't miss any classes, Darcy," she confesses. "I'm only back this semester because of scholarships and a small loan. I'm not going to screw this up."

I hug her. She's not very touchy feely, but I know standing up to her father and being cut off monetarily has been stressing her out. I won't let her go through this semester alone.

* * *

Even though I'm excited about my studies this year there's a bundle of nerves building within my stomach. I'm not ready to be around Derrick again after seeing him for the first time in six months last year.

I place my notebooks on top of each other neatly along with a pouch of pens that I keep with me at all times. I swear I have every color of the rainbow within that zippered bag. But, you never know when you'll need different colors to take notes. After I get them exactly how I like them, I slide them into my backpack.

"Does this look okay?" Cami asks as she barges into our dorm room.

"Ummmm." I take a moment to look her over. "I've only ever seen you in a dress once." That was the night I was forced into a blind date with the evil person I don't even want to name. Today, she has on a simple black skater dress.

"Well," she groans. "It's hot as hell out there and I don't feel like wearing shorts. This was my only other option."

"You look cute. Travis is going to be one happy guy when he sees you."

"I hope so." She falls onto her bed, swooning like some princess in a story. "I mean, I know I saw him over summer break, but it'll be nice being able to see him whenever I want without Tonya's parents playing twenty questions on him."

I snort. "If that's the worst of your problems, you have it made."

Cami sits up, shoving her notebooks into her backpack without any sort of organization, and I cringe. "You know the likelihood of you and Derrick having a class together is pretty slim, right?"

"But, there's always the chance that I'll run into him around campus," I sigh. "Plus, there's the fact that you're dating his best friend. That pretty much guarantees that I'm going to see him more than I want to."

"I promise I will try to limit any interaction you two may have," she laughs. "Geez, I feel like I'm trying to keep two toddlers in separate corners."

"I'm sorry, I don't mean to be a pain in the ass. But he broke my heart, and I still haven't gotten over it." I lean against the wall, hoping it will give me the support I need. Cami doesn't get it. Until Travis, she was casual with guys. I've never been that way. Even though I no longer wear the geeky shirts, that insecure nerd is still hidden within the depths of me.

"Can't you just hold my hand through the day?" I whine.

"That would be impossible. We aren't even on the same track as far as courses go."

"Fine," I huff. "If you're going to be mean, I'm going to class."

"Don't be a crybaby about it," she argues. "Everything will be okay. I promise."

* * *

Everything is *not* okay. It's the exact opposite. Sitting front and center in my first class of the day is Derrick. Cami's future predicting skills need some serious work. So much for a slim chance we'd have a class together.

It takes everything in me not to turn right back around and run out of this room. Call me a coward. I don't really care. Walking on a bed of nails would be easier than facing him again.

Instead, I straighten my shoulders, lift my chin, and walk to a seat a few rows up from him like the badass I hope I'm portraying. If I'm lucky, he won't even see me.

But, of course, I'm not lucky. Why on earth would I be? Him being here shows just how much Fate hates me. As soon as my butt hits the chair, I glance up, and he's staring right at me.

Derrick gathers his things. I'm presuming to move closer to me, and I just can't. Not today. I grab my bag and haul ass out the door, like the devil is on my heels.

derrick

WATCHING Darcy hightail it out of the classroom is a punch to the gut. I didn't expect to share a class with her. It was just a happy coincidence. I know I hurt her when I didn't show up to our date last summer, but I had my reasons. And, I would have explained them to her if only she would have given me a chance.

But, she didn't. Not when I called. And, not when I texted. She just disappeared. She ghosted me without a second thought. I really liked her, and I still do. Even after that disastrous blind date with Travis and Cami. When she was glaring at me like she wished she could torture me.

I also may have laid on the sweetness a little too much that night. I knew it would get under her skin. Knew it would piss her off. But I didn't care because she was at least acknowledging that I exist. That somewhere buried deep beneath all the loathing, she might actually still care about me.

Or, I may be imagining it all. Maybe she didn't care about me, as much as I did her, back then. I just need a chance to find out. A chance to tell her I'm sorry.

My thoughts of Darcy are interrupted when the professor walks into the room. He doesn't bother introducing himself, or taking attendance, he just jumps right into his lecture. I can already tell this year is going to be hell in this class.

I really shouldn't have been quite so lazy last year. Getting my body ready to try out for the basketball team has been brutal. I'm busting my ass to make sure I secure a spot, but I forgot how draining it can be. Don't get me wrong, I didn't *not* play last year, but the games weren't so labor intensive. Just a few guys getting together to shoot the ball around.

Sweat drenches my body, and I want nothing more than to go back to the dorm room I share with Travis, and collapse on the bed. But, I can't. I still have assignments to get started on. Who the hell gives homework on the first day of classes?

That's when it hits me. This isn't high school anymore. It may be a little early to be pushing myself to the brink. But I also have the disadvantage of coming in a year later than the rest of the guys my age. I *need* to prove to the coaches, and rest of the players, that I'm cut out to be on this team.

A ball slams me in the chest. "Rhodes, get your head out of the clouds."

Shit, I completely spaced out. Too worried about what I need to do instead of actually doing it. "Sorry, Bentley."

"It's all good." He holds his arms out waiting for me to pass him the ball that's slowly bouncing away from my feet. "But, you're not going to make the cut if you don't start paying attention."

There's nothing like being called out by the guy who's offered to help. I have to do better. I have to stay focused.

The image of Darcy running out of the classroom this morning pops into my thoughts. I shake it off, even though it pains me. Right now, isn't the time to be thinking about her. Not when I have something to prove to this college.

I unlock the door and shove it open. Showering would probably be a good decision right now, but I just want to flop onto my bed for a bit. Even if it is super uncomfortable, and nothing like the soft bed I have at home. Just to rest before I start tackling my assignments.

A shriek comes from Travis's side of the room. "Shit,"

I yell. "I'm sorry." I stumble over my feet trying to get back into the hallway.

Five minutes have gone by before I hear Travis through the door. "It's safe to come in now."

"Dude, what the hell?"

"Did you not see the sock on the door?" Travis asks.

"Yeah," I mumble. "Is that supposed to mean something?"

"It means...the room is currently occupied and you shouldn't come barging in," Cami rolls her eyes. "What did you think it was there for?"

"I thought some douchebag put it there as some kind of prank."

Travis laughs. "You can definitely tell you're new to this whole college thing."

Cami is sitting beside him, hand over her mouth, trying to contain her giggles. "You're such a newb."

"Whatever," I snap. "So, can I stay in our room, or do I need to leave?"

"You can stay," Cami says, voice softening. She must be able to see how exhausted I am.

"Thanks."

"Soooo," Cami drawls. "A little birdie told me that you and Darcy share a class together."

The first real smile since the grueling practice takes over my face. "I'm assuming by little birdie, you mean Darcy."

"I'm not at liberty to say." She mimes zipping her lips

closed, twisting her fingers once she gets to the end, and throwing away an imaginary key.

"It's not hard to figure out," I snort. "Did she say anything else about me?"

She shrugs, picking at the edge of her nail. "Nothing good, that's for sure." She pauses. "What happened between the two of you anyway?"

I'm surprised Darcy hasn't said anything to her about that night. Or, had a Derrick bashing session. But, I also don't want to overstep my boundaries in their friendship. "Just a misunderstanding."

"It must have been some misunderstanding. Darcy is generally a happy person until your name is brought up. Plus, anytime she sees you she gets this evil glint in her eye. Like she wishes she could set you on fire and watch you burn."

Ouch. That is not a visual I need. It does make it obvious that I at least have some sort of place in her thoughts, though. I just need them to shift from villain to hero.

"Do you think you could help me get close to her again? Close enough to actually talk to her?" I ask. I'll beg if I have to, but I hope it doesn't come down to that.

Cami bites her bottom lip, doubt swirling in her eyes. "I don't know."

Travis is shaking his head vehemently. "No. I'm not getting dragged into whatever is going on between the two of you. If her reaction the last time she saw you is any indication, us getting in the middle isn't going to make it any better."

"But, you know what happened wasn't my fault." I whine. And yes, I'm whining like a petulant child. He didn't even know about Darcy until after the blind date. I only told him because I had to explain why she hates my guts. That summer was hard on him dealing with all the shit his mom threw at him. I didn't want to bother him with my dating life.

"You *know* what happened, and you haven't told me." Cami jumps off the bed. "Some boyfriend you are."

She's kidding, mostly. It is reassuring that he hasn't said anything since they tell each other every little thing. I don't think one breathes without the other knowing.

"It wasn't my story," Travis shrugs. "It wasn't my place to say anything."

"Whatever," she punches him lightly on his shoulder. "Just for that, though, I'm in." A wide grin spreads across her face. It's actually kind of creepy. "It's been a while since I've played cupid."

Yes. Now, I just need to figure out what I'm going to do to sweep her off her feet and into my arms.

darcy

THE NUMBER of people that have come into Roasted tonight is insane. The mornings are for the corporate types. Getting their coffee fix before a long day in the office. But, nights? The crowd turns into students needing a caffeine fix to get through their assignments or get as much studying done as possible.

It's those students that fill the seats tonight. It's only the second day of the semester. How much could they have already been assigned? I shouldn't say much, though. My course load this year is full of science and math classes.

One biology class might be cut. I don't know if I can spend an entire semester in the same class as Derrick without wanting to throat punch him. A tiny part of me wants to know why he's taking the class. He never mentioned any kind of dreams or aspirations when we dated that summer.

I also never asked. Too wrapped up in a guy showing me attention. Too excited about being pursued for the first time in my life. It's never happened before and I didn't know what to do. I gave him my heart. Trusted that he would keep it safe.

Instead, he demolished it. Put it through a shredder until it came out in tiny, uneven slivers. Now...I'm not sure I'll ever trust a guy again. I *know* I'll never be able to trust him again. Not unless he's miraculously done a complete turnaround. Maybe not even then.

Someone bumps into me as I'm cleaning the recently vacated table in front of the window. When I turn, it's Cami standing behind me, staring out the window filled with the night sky. She notices that she's caught my attention and nods toward the other side of the window before sauntering off to Travis's table for the twentieth time tonight.

Derrick is standing opposite me, watching. My lips part and I inhale. How long has he been standing there? He has on long black basketball shorts and a tank top. A slight sheen covers his skin. He must have been playing before I caught his attention.

Everything I felt when he first approached me start bubbling up. The giddiness, butterflies flitting around in my stomach, and the exhilaration of being wanted begin to surface.

He lifts a hand into the air giving me a small wave, and he looks almost boyish. Unsure of himself. Then the smirk that I fell for appears on his face and I can see hope lighting up his eyes.

I force all those walls that are begging to lift back down. Remember how I cried in my car until I gathered my composure enough to drive home and not have my parents questioning what happened. The times I cried myself to sleep because I didn't understand why he seemed so excited one day and then ditched me the next.

That's not going to happen again. Not if I have a say about it. So, instead of waving back at him. I roll my eyes and scowl. He's not getting back in. I won't make the same mistake twice.

"Why didn't you wave back?" My best friend's voice comes from behind me. How in the world does she do that creepy ninja stealth move? I really need to learn so I can sneak up on my brother, Bradley, and scare the crap out of him.

I shrug. "I don't want him in my life. It's as simple as that."

"Why won't you tell me what happened with the two of you?"

"Because," I say. "I don't want to revert back to being that naive girl anymore. I'm not who I used to be."

She wants to argue. I can see it in the way she pulls her shoulders back. But she surprises me. "I'll let you slide. For now. Don't think I won't pry the story out of you."

"Good luck," I singsong. She'll need it because the

only way I will ever tell her what happened is if there is alcohol involved.

* * *

Walking into class Wednesday morning is the hardest thing I've done in a long time. I don't want to be here. And, I definitely want to keep my interactions with Derrick to a minimum.

Maybe I can act like he doesn't exist. Not that it worked before. Anytime I'm in the same space as him, I feel his presence. Feel him looking at me. I get goose-bumps when it happens, and I don't want him to get any sort of reaction, except pissed off, from me.

I take a quick peek inside the room to see if he's there yet. I don't see him, and walk in. Should I sit in the front like I've always done in all of my classes? Or, find a seat in the back so he won't notice me?

There are a lot of open seats in the front. He could easily sit next to me and I wouldn't be able to do anything about it without causing a disruption. A few rows from the back of the classroom is one seat that hasn't been taken. I'm not a huge fan of sitting next to people, since they tend to distract me, but I'll take one for the team if it means not being near him.

My notebook is opened up in front of me. A pen and highlighter lying next to it. I read the first couple of chapters in the textbook since I have no idea what they covered in class on Monday.

Two people walk in just before the class starts. Derrick, and I'm assuming the professor. I'm a little shocked when he jumps right into the lecture. He doesn't even glance at the students attending his class. He walks straight to the white board and starts writing down terms.

Derrick, however, makes his way to the back of the room and sits directly behind me. Next time I'm sitting in the back corner.

The knowledge that he's just one backward glance away distracts me more than I would like to admit. Trying to pay attention to the lecture is not an easy task.

When the professor takes a moment to look at his agenda, Derrick taps me on the shoulder. I do my best to ignore it, but then he slides a sheet of paper towards me.

At first, I think it's something completely ridiculous, but it's the notes from class on Monday. Why would he do that? Especially since I shoot him death glares anytime I see him.

Following along with the lecture is only a tad bit easier since I read the textbook, but there are definitely things I missed in the last class. Right this second, I'm grateful that Derrick thought of me by making a copy of the notes he took. Is this some ploy to get me to talk to him? Or, is he just doing it out of kindness.

I won't find out until after class is over. The squeak of the dry erase marker moving quickly over the board snaps my attention back to the lecture.

It feels like the class is taking forever. The monotone

voice coming from the front of the room is making me fall asleep. Derrick may not end up being the reason I drop this class. If this is what I have to look forward to for the rest of the semester, I'm going to have to take a couple of shots of espresso before I leave the morning shift just to focus.

Finally, the professor stops talking and returns to his podium. A sigh of relief breaks through my lips. I've always been one to love all of my classes, but this is on a whole new level of boring. But I need this class, so I'll suffer through it.

I slowly pack away my things, trying to give the other students plenty of time to leave the room. Derrick hasn't left the room yet, either. I'm not sure what to say to him since he gave me his notes. I don't know where to classify him in regard to friends, or enemies.

"Hey," he whispers from behind as I pick up my bag and stand. His hands are shoved in his pockets and his backpack is slung haphazardly on his shoulder. It's not even completely zipped up. He's going to end up losing something.

"Um, hi," I say to his feet. I can't look at his face. Can't risk staring into his eyes, and inevitably fall for him all over again. Nope, that's not what is going to happen. Staring at his feet is so much easier.

"Dar," he says his pet name for me, lifting my chin up until his face is all I can see. "My eyes are up here."

"I'm perfectly aware of that," I snap.

The smirk lifting up one corner of his mouth shows just how much he's taking pleasure in knowing how uncomfortable I am. I feel like I'm staring at a new version of him. The guy I met when I was eighteen was sweet, charming, and didn't like to test what he could do to get under my skin.

I take a moment to study him. And, I mean *really* study him. He still looks the same, more or less. Same dark hair that's longer on the top than it is on the sides. Same annoying as hell smile. The only difference is he's not as confident as he once was. He's unsure of himself. I don't know if that has to do with him coming in a year later than the rest of us. Or, if I'm somehow at the heart of it.

His brows furrow. Dang it, I must have been staring too long. That's exactly the kind of impression I wanted to leave him. Not really, but I'll have to make do with the awkwardness.

"Thanks for the notes," I push a stray piece of hair behind my ear.

"Not a problem." Shuffling his feet, he runs his hand through his hair. Both of us at a loss of words. I need to get out of here before things get weird.

I glance at my watch, feigning surprise at the time. "I need to go. My next class starts soon."

He opens his mouth as if he is going to say something but closes it after a second thought. I walk out of the classroom this time, not quite as in a hurry as I was on the first day. A quick glance back, and he's still watching me walk away.

A small smile graces my lips, but quickly disappears. One small act of kindness shouldn't have my heart drumming against my chest. I need to process my feelings before I see him again.

derrick

GUNSHOTS RING out through my headphones. I'm pushing aside my homework for the night to play video games. It's also a nice distraction from Darcy. There's so much I wanted to say before she said she had to go.

I was going to apologize. Maybe explain what happened that night. But, she looked so uncomfortable just being around me, I let her use whatever excuse she needed to leave.

I didn't miss the way she openly studied me. I only wish I knew what she was thinking. I'm sure it wasn't anything good, but one can hope.

"Dammit," I mutter as yet another guy on my squad is taken out. "Get your shit together guys."

"Dude," a voice comes from behind me. "You know it's just a game, right?"

Travis is alone, shockingly, throwing his bag onto his

bed. He doesn't bother scooting it over before his body lands on the bed.

Pressing pause I take off my headphones. "I know, but it'd be nice if they played like they give a damn."

"You take that way too seriously."

"Whatever, man." I turn the game off. It's not like I'm going to get any XP points playing with the morons on tonight. "Where's Cami? The two of you are usually attached at the hip."

"I had to tutor tonight, so she took the opportunity to try to get ahead on her classes."

"Why in the world would she want to do that?"

"Because," he sighs. "She's here on a scholarship and student loans. She doesn't want to do anything that could screw it up."

"Makes sense, I guess." I pause. Should I ask him if Cami has talked to Darcy. I mean she seemed almost nice at the end of class today. It was a nice departure from the scowls that are constantly directed toward me.

"Before you ask, no I don't know if Cami has talked to her."

"How did you even know that's what I was going to ask?" I say in mock innocence. "I could be wondering what the weather is supposed to be tomorrow."

"We live in Texas, dumbass. It's going to be hot for a long time." Travis throws one of his pillows at my head, barely missing. Instead, it hits the corner of the tiny television we have, and I have to jump to keep it from tumbling to the ground. "Besides, you had that lovesick puppy look you always have when you're thinking about her."

I toss the pillow back at him, hitting him in the face. "I recall a certain someone walking around with that same expression."

"I don't know what you're talking about."

"Dude, you still have that look on your face anytime her name is mentioned, and y'all have been together for almost six months."

Travis doesn't respond. He throws his pillow to the side and quickly stands. "Want to go shoot some hoops?"

Any other day I would be jumping at the chance to hit the courts. But as hard as Bentley has worked me lately, a basketball is the last thing I want to see. "I'd rather not."

"Wow," he shakes his head. "I never thought I'd see the day where you wouldn't want to play."

"If you'd been practicing as much as I have, you'd want to be lazy, too." I vacate the chair I've been sitting in for the past few hours while getting my ass handed to me on the video game. Grabbing my backpack, I walk to my bed debating whether I want to pull out my notebooks and laptop.

I should really take this opportunity to get some studying done since I didn't pay any attention during my first lecture this morning. I know Darcy picked her seat to try to keep away from me. I'm not stupid, but I'm also not one to throw away an opportunity. The second I saw the chair behind her was empty I made my move.

I also knew she wouldn't have time to switch seats because I rushed past our professor when he was on his way to the classroom. Purposefully hesitating by the door until he was close enough that a seat change wasn't possible.

Travis's voice breaks into my thoughts. "Since you asked about Cam talking to Darcy, I assume you've had some sort of interaction with her today."

"You would assume correct." I can't help the grin that takes over my face. Even when she's hates my guts, I can't keep myself from hoping that she'll give me another chance.

"And?" He questions.

"And, she still pretty much hates me." I pause. "I think."

Quick beeps come from the microwave sitting on a shelf on Travis's side of the room. A few seconds after he's started it, the buttery smell of popcorn fills the room. I hope he's sharing. I've just realized that I haven't eaten since right after my last class before practice.

"Earth to Derrick," he waves a hand in front of my face.

"You burnt the popcorn." I mutter in response.

"No I didn-," he breaks off. "Shit."

He grabs the bag and runs out of the room. I'm not a hundred percent sure where he's taking it, but if I had my guess it's the bathroom down the hall.

Heavy footsteps come down the hallway, until a frustrated Travis appears in the door. "What good is the damn popcorn setting if it's just going to burn every-thing in the bag?"

"You have to listen to the popping," I say. "Once it slows down, it's time to take it out."

He's rummaging around in the small cabinet where he hides all his snacks. I don't know why he hides them. I'm the only other person that is always in the room besides Cami. Before that it was only him. Does he think someone's going to come in and steal everything he has squirreled away in there?

"That was the last bag," he whines.

"Want me to order a pizza?" I know he can't really afford to eat out. He's a master at budgeting money for the semester. I guess that's what happens when you have an unreliable mother, and never know if you're going to have the money to eat. I tap on the app for the closest pizza place. Already ordering before he responds.

"Sure." I'm hoping he's dropped the conversation about Darcy, but he picks up right where we left off. "So, what happened? Why do you *think* Darcy still hates you? You knew before, what changed?"

I rub the back of my neck. I'm not quite sure how to answer because in reality, I have no idea. She's not the type to let one good deed make up for being done wrong. I remember when she told me about the grudge she held against her brother for six months just for putting a piece of cellophane across her door as a prank.

"I gave her my notes?" It's more question than an answer, but it's the only thing I can think of. Travis's quizzical look seems to agree that it's odd. "She ran out of class on Monday. I copied my notes and gave them to her." Blowing out a breath I continue. "It was weird. She seemed to let down her guard a little when she thanked me, but then she made an excuse to leave as soon as things felt awkward. That's why I wondered if Cami said something to her."

"Not that I know of," Travis replies. "Maybe she still carries a torch for you but is too scared to admit, or act on, it."

"That's what I'm banking on." I lean back against the wall abandoning my homework. It's not going to get done anyway. "I just need to break her walls down a little bit more."

"I'm going to ask you a question you once asked me."

I've asked him a lot of questions. I'm not entirely sure which one he's referring to. I nod for him to continue.

He sits in the chair I left moments before and spins it until he's facing me straight on. "Is she worth whatever heartbreak is bound to come out of this little game you're playing to win her back?"

"More than you know." I reply, just as we get a buzz from downstairs. Our pizza is here.

Travis rushes downstairs to get it while I let the question run through my mind. Darcy is worth everything. Even if I have to walk through a wall of flames, and get singed, I'll do whatever it takes to prove to her that she means the world to me.

darcy

THE RECREATION CENTER is eerily quiet as I walk down the hall to one of the smaller rooms used for various classes. I assumed this place would be teeming with students since it's Saturday. But it's practically a ghost town, making the search for an empty room to set up my yoga mat much easier.

It's been a stressful first week back at Hilltown. Between work, school, and my still confused feelings about Derrick, I need to decompress and find my center. Yoga is the only thing that helps me accomplish that.

It's something I picked up when I was still in high school. I was so busy pushing myself to excel at everything I almost gave myself a nervous breakdown. Mom took me to one of her classes, and I fell in love with it. It's calming, and pretty much the only time I can be alone with my thoughts. Maybe today's session will bring me some clarity on what to do about Derrick. Or, at least help me figure out how I feel about him.

Normally I would move through the positions on my own until I feel comfortable, but today I need a little guidance. I find a small room at the end of the hallway that will suit my purposes. I lay my mat out in the middle and set up my iPad to the yoga instructor I follow on YouTube. The windows are uncovered and sunlight streams in. Lighting up the room enough so I don't have to turn on the actual light. It's serene and perfect for what I need out of today's session.

The instructor's soothing voice guides me through breathing and stretching out my muscles. I'm a little shaky during the stretches. Forcing my achy muscles to go through the motions until I feel a slow welcome burn. Feeling the stress, I'm carrying slowly begin to float away.

I deepen my breaths and try my best to clear my thoughts. But Derrick keeps popping up, refusing to be pushed away. The rest of the week went by without any animosity. We were even cordial to each other.

I didn't freak out when he found a seat next to me. That in itself is a huge improvement. Don't get me wrong, I didn't try to initiate any conversations with him. He's not forgiven for standing me up. But, when he would say hello, I would respond.

I think back to that night and feel the sadness I felt seep into my bones. I was a different girl back then, though. Now, I'm the bubbly, happy girl. It's not a facade, either. After everything happened with Derrick, I promised myself I wouldn't be the shy girl anymore. I would put myself out there, make friends, and not hold myself back.

I also completely revamped my wardrobe. I brought a few of my favorite nerdy t-shirts with me, but they are shoved in the back of my closet and only come out when nobody is around to witness them. Now, my closet is full of dresses, rompers, and oversized sweaters for the winter. I'm not sure what anyone would think if I wore a Doctor Who shirt to class.

Tension begins building in my shoulders again. Not because I hate the person I am now, but because I'm a little sad that I've hidden the things that I enjoy. Nobody knows that about me, except for one person. Derrick.

I pause the video. I've already almost completely lost my focus, but I need to get it back. My breaths deepen as I center myself once again, finally pushing all thoughts of Derrick and who I used to be out of my head.

I'm working my way into downward dog when a faint bouncing catches my attention. It's repetitive, and just loud enough to break my concentration. Huffing out a sigh, I stand. There's no point in trying to finish this yoga session. I roll up my mat, tuck it under my arm and grab the iPad.

Rolling my neck back and forth, I notice the tension I've been feeling there has lessened. Not much, but enough for me to be somewhat happy about my short exercise. My legs are a little wobbly from staying in a couple of positions too long, but the feeling will pass soon enough.

The sun is still shining when I walk out of the room and start down the hall toward the front of the recreation center. The closer I get to the gym, the louder the bouncing of the ball becomes. I almost pass the door up, but the figure standing at the free-throw line catches my attention.

Derrick is standing there, getting his body into position to shoot the ball. I should leave, I know I should. But I don't. I lean against the door and watch, like some sort of stalker. When we dated, I spent so many nights watching him practice in the driveway. In awe at the way his body moved, and how he knew exactly what needed to be corrected when he missed a shot. Afterward we would lie on the hood of his car while music drifted out of the speakers and talk about everything and nothing.

He lifts his arms, the ball leaving his hands and landing in the basket with a swish. Nothing but net. I may have studied up on basketball while we were dating so I wouldn't look like a moron if I ever watched him play an actual game.

The ball hits the floor, bounces a couple of times, and begins to roll...straight toward me. He doesn't notice me at first, too focused on trying to get the ball before it rolls into the hallway.

Then he looks up. "Darcy?" It comes out as a question. "What are you doing here?"

My cheeks warm. "I just finished a yoga workout and saw you in here while I was on my way out."

"Do you feel better?"

Huh. "Why would I feel bad?"

"I just remember you doing yoga when you were stressed." He shrugs his shoulders as if him remembering that isn't a big deal. "So, I figured maybe you would do the same thing now."

"Oh." I'm not sure what else to say. I'm still kind of shocked he remembered something from back then. "Um, yeah. I've been stressed this week with work, school, and everything else."

I was so close to saying "you," but I have enough common sense to think before I speak. The both of us are silent, staring at each other. Not sure what to say, just being present in our own little bubble of awkwardness.

The yoga mat wedged under my arm begins to slip. I bend and bounce trying to readjust it at the same time Derrick bends and reaches for it. Our heads collide as the mat falls to the floor.

Hand to my head, rubbing the knot I'm pretty sure isn't going to be pretty, I stand back up. His reaction mirrors mine. We make eye contact and burst out laughing. Seeing him in his element and the thoughtfulness of him trying to help me twice this week, lessens my pent-up anger just a smidge.

"Are you okay?" He's still trying to get his laughter under control.

"Yeah, you?"

"I'm great, actually."

"Why?" How can he be great when I'm pretty sure we just gave each other massive headaches?

"You're talking to me."

My face heats, again, and I'm pretty sure I'm blushing. "I-I just watched you practice while on my way out. It's really not that big of a deal."

"Considering you've treated me with disdain since I showed up where you work last semester...I would say this is a pretty big deal."

"Well, when you put it like that." The sad thing is, I can see his point. Anytime he's even tried talking to me I've shut him down or ran away. Being bitchy and running away were easy options for me.

I've held a grudge against him for so long that I haven't even been able to be in his presence without being awful to him. If my mom saw how I was acting she would be so disappointed.

"Can we talk? While you're here?" He whispers, voice barely loud enough for me to hear. I jumped Cami's butt last year when she wouldn't talk things out with Travis. But yet, here I am, doing the same thing to Derrick. I am such a hypocrite.

"Sure." I walk toward the set of bleachers lining the wall. I have a feeling I might need to sit for whatever he's about to tell me.

There's still not a single soul in this recreation center, and it's deafeningly quiet. Staring at my feet, I sit down, noticing my yoga mat is still over by the door. I almost move to get it. If only to buy me a little bit more time. Just enough to get my breathing under control and my heart prepared to possibly be shattered again.

"Dar," he puts his finger under my chin, guiding me toward his eyes. "Look at me." He doesn't remove his hand when my gaze captures his. His thumb moves gently over my cheek then down to my jaw. It's something he used to do *then*, and my breath hitches.

"You wanted to talk?" I ask softly.

He removes his hand. Even though it's hot outside, I miss the warmth of him touching me. Soothing me when he knows I'm uncomfortable. This is why I didn't want to be nice to him. Letting him in just the slightest bit breaks down my barriers. How am I supposed to guard my heart if he's going to keep doing things like that?

"That night I didn't show?" I open my mouth to say something, but he doesn't give me a chance. "It wasn't because I didn't want to be there. I would have preferred being there than where I was."

"Where were you?" I ask, the anger and hurt I felt that night returning. "You didn't call or text. I waited there for almost an hour waiting."

"I know, and I'm sorry," he sighs. "I tried calling you as soon as I could but you wouldn't answer. You didn't give me a chance to explain."

Fighting back tears I cross my arms over my chest. As if that will shield me from what he has to say. "Now's your chance," I bite out.

"I'm trying to Darcy, but you aren't exactly making it easy."

I jump to my feet. I need to get out of here. If he isn't going to get to the point there's no reason for me to even be here. I shouldn't have stopped. As soon as I saw him in here alone, I should have marched right past the door.

Halfway to the entrance, I feel a hand around my wrist. "Darcy, wait."

I turn, but I can't look at him. Can't let him know that he still gets to me more than he should.

"Gramps was in the hospital." He lets go of my wrist. "He passed away right before I was supposed to meet you. I didn't think to grab my phone before we rushed to the hospital to be with my grandma. I saw your text when we got back."

I can't look at him for different reasons now. Tears stream down my face. Not because he broke my heart that night. But because I feel like shit for how I've treated him. I didn't answer his call. I wasn't there for him when he needed me. Instead, I was too mired in my own emotions that I didn't even give him a chance.

"Darcy?"

A sob breaks free. "I'm so sorry."

He pulls me into a hug. "It's okay."

"No," I choke. "It isn't. I've been horrible to you."

He pats my back waiting for me to calm down. Even now, he's consoling me. Making sure I'm okay after acting the way that I have. He lost someone. Someone he was close to. I remember the stories he would tell me about his Gramps taking him fishing. I knew he was having health issues, but I didn't realize they were so severe.

"I'm not going to lie, it sucked when you ignored me." He stops patting me and bends down until he can see my face. "But I've only ever wanted to tell you why I didn't show up."

"Thank you," I sniff, "for telling me."

This information means I have no reason to be angry at him. But still, I need to process my feelings. If I didn't think he would follow me, I'd go back to that vacant room for another yoga session. I really need some calm right now, or maybe just someone to talk to.

I glance at my watch. Cami should be off work soon. She'll know what to do. And if she doesn't, she'll call Tonya. "I have to go."

Turning I take off toward the door as fast as I can without looking like I'm running, even though that's exactly what I'm doing.

"There aren't any classes today," he yells to my retreating form.

I'm almost to my dorm when I realize I've left my yoga mat. I turn to go back but decide against it. Derrick will be there, waiting for me to return. I have another one I can use. Right now, I plan on binge watching *Buffy* until Cami gets home so I can unload everything on her.

derrick

SHE BAILED ON ME...AGAIN. Why does she keep doing that? I figured I could talk to her more after I told her why I didn't make it to our date. I held her while she sobbed, but she still freaking left me.

My gaze travels to the floor where her yoga mat is still taking up space. I pick it up and wait. She'll come back for it. No way she's going to leave her favorite mat here. At least, I don't think she will. But, Darcy isn't the same girl I dated back then. It's not a bad thing, just different.

I remember all the times she rolled it out in my driveway going through a workout while I practiced. A few times the basketball would roll toward her, knocking her off balance. Instead of continuing with her workout, she would pull me down as soon as I was close enough to grab the ball. Refusing to let me get back to playing. I didn't mind. It was her playfulness in those moments when we were alone that made me fall for her. It also made me wonder why she wasn't already taken.

Twenty minutes pass by. Is she getting her payback on me standing her up? I mean, I understand why she would, even with my reasons. But I'm hoping more than anything that she will come back. Even over a year later, I've still got it bad for her.

Ten more minutes have passed, and my shoulders slump in defeat. I stare at the door with the resignation that she's not coming for her favorite mat. She's cut her losses, and me right along with them.

One would think that's enough to persuade me to stop bugging her. To *finally* let her go. But it's not. The yoga mat is leverage. Another chance for me to see her this weekend. What kind of person would I be if I didn't return property to its rightful owner?

* * *

"Why do you have a yoga mat?" Travis raises his eyebrows and points to said mat.

"Darcy left it at the rec center." Leaning the mat against the wall by my bed, I turn with a huge grin.

"I'm guessing you talked?" He holds a bag of popcorn that is definitely not burnt.

I reach my hand in grabbing as much as I can hold. A few kernels drop from my hand as I pull it out. Small white puffs littering the floor. "We did."

"Seriously?" Travis points to the mess on the floor. "You're just going to leave that there?"

"I'll get it in a minute." I shovel as many pieces of popcorn as I can into my mouth. "Don't you want to know how it went with Darcy?" I mumble around the food in my mouth.

"Why don't you tell me while you clean that up?"

"Geez, you sound like Mom."

Travis rolls his eyes and taps his foot. He's been around my mom way too long. Their actions are so similar it's uncanny.

"Fine," I grumble, getting off my bed. I pick up the few pieces that I dropped and toss them in the trash can.

I plop back onto my bed and stare at the ceiling. They are gray and dingy. When was the last time they updated these dorms? They should definitely consider it if they want to keep student morale high. Nobody can help but get depressed staring at these dull walls all the time. No amount of colorful decoration will help this situation.

"Yo, Derrick," Travis snaps his fingers in front of my face. "Are you ever going to tell me what happened with Darcy?"

"Oh, yeah" I shake away thoughts of the boring dorm room. "So, she watched me practice today. Then I actually got her to speak to me without running off, mostly."

"Mostly?"

"Yep. I finally got my chance to tell her what happened last summer, and she broke down in my arms."

"And?"

"Then she bailed," I smile.

Travis looks confused. His eyebrows almost touch as he tries to puzzle out what I've just said. "If she ran, again, why are you smiling?"

I nod toward the yoga mat leaning against the wall. "Because, my friend, she left that behind."

"It's a cheap yoga mat."

"Maybe, but it's the one she always used when we were together. She may have another one. But, this one is her favorite. Since I have it, I can return it to her. Giving me another chance to talk to her."

Travis sits in the lone chair at the desk, spinning it around a couple of times before stopping it to face me. "And, what? You're just going to hand it over in class Monday morning?"

"Nope," I pop the p with a little more exaggeration than needed. "I'm going to take it to her tomorrow."

"What if she works?"

My smile widens. "That's where you come in."

"Oh, no. I told her I didn't want to get in the middle of this."

"Then give me Cami's number. She's more than happy to help me win back Darcy's good graces."

"Uh uh, that's not happening."

"Then I suggest you text Cami and ask her if Darcy is working tomorrow." I gesture toward the phone sitting on the desk. "Then let me kick your ass in *Ghost Recon*."

He bats his eyes. "Well, when you put it so sweetly."

"Nobody likes a smartass," I retort.

"Well," he types out a message on his phone, hopefully to Cami. "One day your half-brained dumbass ideas are going to come back to haunt you."

"It's genius." The controller for the PlayStation is just out of my reach, and I have to sit up to grab it.

"If you say so, man." He pauses for a moment, no longer tapping at his phone. "Have you ever considered that maybe she just isn't interested anymore, and you're making her uncomfortable?"

"Nobody goes out of their way to avoid someone as much as she has me if they don't still have some sort of feelings."

The sound of a message being sent is loud as Travis presses the button. "Just remember, this has a lot of potential for heartbreak on both sides, and Cami and I will be stuck in the middle."

"Noted." I press the middle button on the controller to turn the system on. "Now, let's play while I come up with the perfect thing to say when I see Dar tomorrow."

darcy

IT'S one of those rare occasions when Cami and I are both off work on the same day. Even better...it's a Sunday. That almost never happens. We tend to work opposite shifts at Roasted on the weekends. Tom finally hired a couple more people, though, and isn't as reliant on us. It's great for our studies, not so much for our pockets.

Buffy is playing on our tiny television. We picked up right where we left off on our binge session last night. She didn't even have to ask me if something was wrong when she walked into the room and saw Buffy kicking ass flickering across the TV in the darkened room. She also didn't press me to talk. Instead, she grabbed a bag of candy from the top shelf of her desk and joined me on her bed.

Cami pauses the DVD. "Who do you ship? Buffy and Angel? Or, Buffy and Spike?"

"Both options are bad for her," I shrug.

"Why do you say that?" She turns to look at me, gauging my reaction to her question.

"Because, they both break her heart at one point or another. She would have been better off without them." I make a grab for the remote to start the show again. "Why should one person go through so much heartache when it can be avoided?"

"What's going on Darcy?" She asks, getting up and putting the remote by the TV, making it harder for me to yank out of her hands. "You've been a totally different person since Der-"

"Don't say his name, please."

"So, this does have to do with him."

"Everything has to do with him. I was fine living in my little happy bubble until he came along and busted it. Now...Now, I don't know what to think."

Placing a hand on my arm, Cami pulls me toward her. "I'm assuming there's been a change of heart?"

"Yes. No. I don't know." I pull my arm from her grasp and roll over to face the open room. "I have new information and I'm not sure what to think anymore."

"Well, maybe I can help."

"Maybe." I roll over toward her again. Remembering the last time, we were in the same situation. Except then...it was me and Tonya trying to pull her from her self-destructive ways. "You're finally going to find out what made me loathe him in the first place."

She rubs her hands together conspiratorially. A wide

grin spreading across her face. "Finally. Do you have any idea how long I've waited for these details?"

"You look entirely too happy about my past misery. Maybe I won't tell you after all."

"You can't take it back. You already said you'd tell me. Now *spill*."

Deep breath in. Hold. Deep breath out. "So, we dated the summer before I came here. Everything was great. We talked or hung out every day. He liked me the way I was. Nerdy and all."

Cami waves her hands in the air. "Wait a minute. Nerdy?"

"Yep. Nerdy. Fandom shirts made up the majority of my wardrobe." I sigh. "Anyway, so we had this sweet and romantic dinner planned for the weekend before I was set to leave. Long story short he stood me up. He didn't call, text, or answer the phone when I tried to call him. It was complete radio silence. And when he tried to call the next day, I ignored him."

"What the hell?" Cami stands and paces the room. No doubt remembering last semester when Travis stood her up and she drank herself into a stupor.

But she's not mad, not exactly. I wonder why she isn't going off in her usual Cami temper tantrum. "Why the change of heart?" She asks, seeming *very* interested in the answer. She must have talked to Derrick or Travis.

"Because he told me why he didn't show up."

"Which was?"

"His grandfather passed away."

She gasps, hands going to her mouth in total surprise. "Are you serious?" I guess they didn't divulge the information to her.

"Yep. Now I feel like a total asshole for harboring this grudge against him for so long. He lost someone he was close to and I didn't give him a chance in hell to explain."

Cami sits next to me on the bed, wrapping her arms around me. All thoughts of watching *Buffy* forgotten. "Don't beat yourself up. You reacted to the information you had at the time. You're human. You're going to make mistakes. You just have to decide what you're going to do about it now."

"Thank you, Captain Obvious."

A knock at the door makes us both jump. I glance at her. "Is Travis supposed to be coming over today?"

She shakes her head, whispering, "No, he had a couple of people he had to tutor today."

The knocking starts again, and we both stare at the door. We normally wouldn't be so spooked, but my emotions are putting me on edge. A quick glance around the room doesn't produce any viable weapons. We should really invest in a bat or something.

Silence comes from the other side of the door. Then there's a sound like someone is leaning against the door.

Finally, a voice I recognize calls my name. "Darcy, if you're in there will you please open the door?"

I breathe a sigh of relief at the sound of Derrick's voice. "Well," I whisper to Cami. "At least we know it's not a murderer."

She laughs quietly, waiting to see if I want to announce our presence. "You really need to lay off those morbid shows you watch."

I shrug. Those shows about murderers and serial killers are interesting. They show just how screwed up a lot of people are. Probably not good for a single college girl to watch, though.

Do I answer the door, or do I wait it out and see if he leaves? It's not like I can avoid him forever. We have class together first thing in the morning. I don't think he'd try to have a serious conversation right before, but you never know with him. He's unpredictable.

The urge to ignore him is strong, but then he speaks again. "Darcy, please open the door." The desperation in his voice pulls at my heartstrings.

Before I realize what I'm doing, my feet are moving toward the door. My hand turning the knob and pulling the door open. Derrick almost falls into me. His forehead most likely on the door as he waited for me to make my decision.

Cami gives me a sheepish grin. "I'm just going to get out of the room for a bit."

"You knew it was him, didn't you?"

"A little birdie may have asked me if you were working today."

"You should definitely consider acting. I bought your whole act." I shoot her a glare, but she just waves me off.

"I'll be back in a bit." She brushes past Derrick and

walks as fast as she can down the hall. No doubt trying to get away from my questioning gaze.

I look up at Derrick. "Travis isn't tutoring anyone today, is he?"

He shakes his head and holds out his arm. Within his hands is my yoga mat.

Once I have it firmly in my own hands, he runs his hand through his hair. "I figured you might want this back."

"Thank you," I whisper.

"I know it's your favorite one."

The small things that he remembers astounds me. I never realized he paid that much attention to me. Maybe he did feel the same way I did. If I'm being honest with myself, he was my first love.

"Can we talk?"

I nod, open the door wider, and motion him inside.

He pauses after he crosses the threshold, not sure where to sit. I point toward my bed, and he sits on the far end, giving me as much space as I need. Debating how close I want to be to him, I finally choose to sit on the opposite end.

"I'm sorry about the way I told you about Gramps." He's rubbing his hands together, a clear sign he's nervous. He's always seemed so confident, and it's reassuring to see that he has insecurities, too. "I didn't mean to blurt it out like that, but you don't usually give me a chance to talk to you about anything that isn't superficial."

"I'm sorry for running off. That seems to be my go-to plan anytime I'm around you."

No longer wringing his hands together, he taps his finger on his chin. "Why is that?"

Ugh, why does he have to question me? "Because," I swallow. "I worry if I'm around you too long, I could easily fall back into an easy relationship with you."

"Would that be so bad?"

"Maybe. Maybe not. But I don't even know you anymore. We haven't seen each other in a long time." I take a deep breath. "And, what if you don't like this new version of me?"

"Not going to lie, I'm not a huge fan of the running off." He reaches across my bubblegum pink bed spread and takes my hand in his. "But I like whatever version of you that you're willing to give me."

My hands may or may not tingle at the contact. Instinctively, I scoot closer to him. Just the tiniest bit. Enough that he notices. And, he squeezes my hand just a bit tighter.

Getting into a relationship with him right now isn't the best idea. I know that. And, I'm sure even though he wants to pick up right where we left off, he knows it, too.

I push down all the warm fuzzies that have invaded my body and listen to reason for once. My hand slides from his, and I can see the disappoint across his face even though he tries not to show it. "How about friends?"

Derrick takes a deep breath and lets it out slowly.

"That wasn't exactly what I was hoping for, but I did say I would take anything you allow me." He holds out his hand, waiting for me to take it. When I do, he gives it firm shake. "Friends."

His hand lingers a beat too long before releasing mine. I'm not sure what to do now. We sit in silence. Him studying my dorm room, and me studying him. His hair is slightly longer, and he still remains hopeful that things will work out. That's one of the things I've always admired about him.

"So," he drawls. "Now that all of that is out of the way and we're friends now, what have you been up to?"

Not sure how to answer this question, I stay quiet. Trying to think about anything exciting that I've done but come up with nothing. "Same thing as usual. Burying myself self in school and work."

He laughs. "Some things never change."

"Nope," I shake my head. "I'm pretty consistent."

"At least you know what you want to do with your life."

"And you don't?" I ask. Basketball was always his main objective, unless that's changed. And, I don't think it has.

"Other than trying to make the basketball team?" He shrugs. "Not really. I'm taking courses for sports medicine, but I'm not sure my heart is in it. It's just something to do while I try to play basketball."

"Who knows, you may end up loving it."

"Maybe."

Another awkward silence takes over us, and I look around my room, wondering what he thinks as he takes it all in. My side of the room is covered in inspirational posters, and artsy prints I've found online. Other than that, it's pretty boring. Is that what I've become? A boring person that only focuses on studying. I've gone to a few parties with Cami, but other than that...I'm home, at work, or in class.

I definitely need to bring some of my former self back. That girl had so much optimism and fun going on new adventures. But what would people think if I let my inner geek out.

My eyes meet Derrick's and I wish I had a peek inside his head to see what he's thinking. To see if I live up to whatever ideals he has of me. He wouldn't be here unless he cared, though. That's the thing I can count on with him, his sincerity.

"I should go," Derrick whispers into the quiet of the room.

"You don't have to." I didn't mean to blurt that out. Even if my feelings about him are all over the place, it feels nice being around him. Just like that summer. It's easy.

The corner of his mouth ticks up, a smile wanting to break through because somehow, he *knows* I still have feelings for him. "I need to study for a couple of classes. Getting on the basketball team isn't going to make all the homework disappear."

"Oh," I stammer, "yeah. I don't want to keep you

from your studies." Gah, I sound like some middle-aged housewife. "If you need any help, let me know."

"I will." He walks to the door, hand on the knob, and pauses. "I'll see you in class tomorrow."

As soon as he closes the door behind him, I sink back onto my bed. Being just friends with him is going to be hard if I don't get my emotions in check. I have a feeling he's not going to stop pursuing more than that, either. Maybe my year is about to get a little less boring.

derrick

THE BALL BOUNCES from the backboard to the rim before hitting the gym floor. Another missed shot. I'm never going to make the team if I don't get my head out of my ass.

But I can't stop replaying my conversation with Darcy yesterday. She won't date me again, which sucks more than I can express. But, she said we could be friends. It's not the outcome I was hoping for, but still something I can work with. It gives me hope that one day she'll want more.

"Rhodes," Bentley barks. "Get your head out of the clouds on the damn ball. You aren't going to make shit if you keep on at this rate."

"Sorry, man." He passes me the ball and I line myself up right outside the three-point line.

I know I won't have time to get my form exact during a game, but this is just to dust off my abilities. Release the ball, I watch it soar through the air to the basket. An almost silent swish meets my ears and I want to let out a whoop of victory at the small success.

"Again," Bentley shouts.

I know he's just trying to help... But, damn, let me celebrate my little accomplishments. It's also why I asked him specifically to train me, though. He doesn't sugarcoat anything because we're *friends*.

My sneakers squeak as I widen my stance. The ball balanced between my hands. Just as I release the ball the gym is flooded with loud music. The momentary distraction makes me miss the basket by at least three feet.

"What the fuck?" I glare at Bentley.

"You need to be prepared for anything. Do you think the fans in the stands are going to be quiet so you can make the perfect shot?"

I shake my head no. I know it's not going to be like that. But, his little stunt with the music scared the hell out of me.

"There are still a few things you need to work on before I deem you ready for tryouts. The most important being your focus." I'm about to argue, but he steams ahead as if I didn't even open my mouth. "Most days your concentration is on point. And, you play like it those days. But others...I can't seem to get you out of your own head. Stop obsessing over the ladies so that you can earn you spot on this team."

Wait. What? I've never said anything to him about Darcy. "How do you know it's about a girl?"

"Because, Rhodes," he slaps me on my back. "They are almost always the reason we lose our damn minds."

He has a point there and seems to be speaking from experience. I've never had a problem keeping my head in the game when Darcy and I were dating. She was mine then, though. I wasn't trying to win her back or get in her good graces.

"I'll do my best to keep my girl drama off the court." I stand taller. Back straight, and shoulders wide, so Bentley knows I'm serious.

"Good," he steps back. "Give me five laps around the gym, then go home."

I salute him. "Yes, sir."

To most that would seem like a smart ass move, but not to him. He's only a few years older than me, but I respect him. He's one of the best senior players on the team. And, the only one willing to help a first-year student, like myself.

He doesn't stay in the gym to make sure I run my laps. He knows I'll do it. If he says jump, I'll ask how high. A spot on this team means more to me than anything. Well, except Darcy.

As I run my laps my thoughts swivel back to her. She's like a drug I can't get enough of. She may have changed since we dated. She definitely traded out her nerdy shirts for more chic clothes, but I still *see* her.

Class this morning wasn't horrible, either. She didn't flinch when I took the desk next to her. Didn't try to hide beneath her curtain of hair. We even joked about how boring our professor is. It was just like the old times, and we were getting back into the groove of being around each other. The only thing missing was making out and holding hands, which I really miss.

But, I can do friends. Totally. For a little while, at least. I'm not saying it's going to be easy because it won't be. Not when I'm envisioning her in my arms, or how soft her lips feel beneath mine.

Groaning, I finish the last lap. Sweat drips down my arms as I walk to the locker room. I need a shower. Preferably a cold one if my thoughts continue in the direction they were taking.

The walk to my dorm room is brutal. The heat beating down on me with every step I take. At this rate I'm going to need another shower by the time I make it to the building.

Cold air blasts from the vents as soon as I open the door to the dormitory. I stand still for a second, letting it cool me down from my walk across campus. The door still wide open earning me a glare from the resident advisor. I don't understand why he's being so bitchy about it. It's not like he just came in from outside.

Letting the door close behind me, I walk toward the elevator bank. Clicking the button until the orange light shows that it's coming down. When the door opens Travis walks out, nearly running right into me.

"Where are you in a hurry to?" I ask. Taking a step back to avoid a collision.

"Shit," Travis grumbles. "Sorry, I didn't see you there. I'm headed to Roasted. I have a tutoring session, but Cami's working so I figured it would be a good location."

"Geez, you can't even go a day without seeing your girl."

His cheeks turn bright red, and I laugh. He's never had someone to be affectionate with since his mom sucked at parenting, so I understand why he gets a little embarrassed when I point it out.

"I'm just playing." I nudge his shoulder. "Do you happen to know if Darcy is working, too?"

"You talk about me, but you're practically stalking the poor girl."

"Eh," I shrug. "We're 'friends' and I happen to be in need of a caffeine fix. I also need to get some studying done."

"I'm not sure if she's working. But you can tag along if you want."

"Awesome." I point at my gym bag. "Just let me throw this in the room and I'll be right down."

The elevator doors have already closed, and I turn to the stairwell.

"Hurry up, I'm already running late." Travis yells as I begin running up the steps. I don't answer because that would take more time.

Luckily, we aren't that far off the ground floor. I pull the key ring out of my pocket and jam it into the knob as soon as I reach our room. My gym bag flies across my side of the room landing somewhere near my pile of dirty laundry. I really need to do some laundry. Or, mail it to my mom so she can do it for me. Because that doesn't scream mama's boy at all. I'll worry about that later.

I scoop up my backpack, and jog back downstairs. Travis is waiting in his car, and motions for me to speed it up. I open the door and welcome the cold air blowing from the dashboard. Hopefully I'm not a sweaty mess when we get to the coffee shop.

darcy

THE LINE of customers wanting their "fix" is nearly out the door! Roasted has been busier than normal and we're not sure why. I am, however, grateful that Tom hired more people. Even with all of us on deck tonight, we can't seem to catch up. I worry we may run out of tables. Maybe I'll suggest adding tables to make a patio out front when we fill up inside. It wouldn't be a horrible investment.

The same grouchy man from the first day of classes is here. He's been coming in more frequently, and it's a little odd. But I keep my mouth shut because he might be going through something nobody else would understand. He could save so much by just making his black coffee at home, but I won't begrudge his choice of coming into Roasted to get his coffee fix.

A bell above the door dings as it opens and I groan. We still have a few hours before we close, and I know I'm going to be too tired to do much of anything else. I have to study for a chemistry quiz tomorrow. The professor is the devil for giving us a quiz on the second week of classes. I mean seriously, who does that?

Soft jazz playing through the speakers can barely be heard over the murmurs of the customers. It's relaxing while working the register. I wish they would put Cami up here sometimes, but she has a habit of getting snippy with the customers. It's not so much that she has an attitude...it's her tone of voice. I love her for it. The people who come in, not so much. Luckily, Tom is understanding and keeps her busy making drinks or the yummy treats we sell.

People's faces are blurring as I take order after order of iced coffee. I don't see him approach the counter so much as *feel* him. Always in tune with Derrick, even when I'm trying to keep things strictly platonic.

"What's a guy gotta do to get a drink around here?" He winks at me as he leans on the counter.

"You know stalking is illegal, right?" The grin on my face telling him that I'm joking.

"I'll have you know I'm here to study." His hand runs through his hair giving it that messy just got out of bed look. "It has absolutely nothing to do with you."

My shoulders slump just the tiniest fraction. Why in the world am I disappointed? Friends, we're just friends. I shouldn't want him going out of his way to see me. But I can't help the flicker of hurt that stabs at me with the knowledge that he's actually not going to pursue anything with me.

Plastering a wide, and absolutely fake, smile on my face I ask, "What can I get you?"

"An iced mocha would be great."

Did I just hear his voice lose some of the enthusiasm it held only moments ago? I shake my head, sure I've imagined it. He just said that he's only here to study. But...I can't help the feeling that he might have been lying about that. That maybe, just maybe, a small part of the reason he came to Roasted is to see me. Even when I've told him that I only want to be friends.

I tell him his total and he hands me a ten-dollar bill. When I try to give him his change, he stuffs it into the tip jar that we all split at the end of the day. I watch him walk away. Hands in his pockets, head down until he finds an empty chair close to Travis. He pulls out a text-book and notepad, preparing to study until his name is called out.

A throat clears at the counter. Dang it. I was too busy ogling him that I didn't see the next person in line come up to the counter. "Sorry, ma'am. What can I get you this evening?"

The massive line has finally dwindled down and I can take my break. I grab a muffin and water out of the display case and search for an empty spot. Only, there's none to be found. Except for one at the table Derrick is currently occupying.

Debating on whether I should just eat in the kitchen, I sigh. My feet take small, careful steps weaving around people until I'm at his table. I set the muffin down before pulling out the chair.

"What are you working on?" I ask as my butt hits the cold, hard wood of the seat.

He looks up in surprise. "Um, I'm going over the notes from this morning's class."

"Do you need any help?"

Derrick shoves his notepad into the book, to mark his place, before he closes the book with a loud thud. "Nope." He looks around at the people milling about. Some standing, or crouching, at tables talking to their friends since there aren't any other chairs available. "Are you off work already?"

"I'm on my break," I answer meekly. Gah, why am I so shy around him all of a sudden. I never used to have this problem when we were dating. In the beginning, sure, because I was still in shock. I never would have imagined a guy like him interested in a nerdy girl like me. But now...Now, I don't know how to act around him. The fine line between coming off friendly and flirty is hard to navigate.

"It's about time." He scoots his chair closer to the table and leans in. "I was beginning to worry you'd work yourself to death."

"Well, even with the extra help, a crowd like this is

hard to manage." Opening my water, I take a sip and set it on the table. "We aren't usually this busy. It's like everyone lost their minds and decided tonight was the night they needed *all* the coffee."

He shrugs. "Maybe they are already feeling the stress of a new semester. I know I wasn't prepared for the amount of work that was going to be thrown at us after the first week of classes."

"Maybe," I mutter, picking small pieces off the muffin and nibbling on them. Do people seriously think college is a walk in the park? It's a lot of work. You get what you put into it. It's not all about partying and hooking up. Though, that is an added bonus when a break is needed.

"Hey," he puts a finger under my chin, lifting my face until I'm looking at him. "We can't all be geniuses like you."

I pull back. "I'm not a genius. I just know how to manage my time. And, I don't like failure."

He chuckles, leaning back into his chair, slouching slightly. "That I know for a fact. It's one of the many things I've always admired about you. You know what you want and work your ass off to get it."

Even after reinventing myself, I'm still unsure how to take compliments. At least, I think it was a compliment. The comment makes it sound like I'm all work and no play, which isn't true at all. Cami can attest to that.

The silence is awkward. I don't know what to say, and I don't think he does either. I glance at my watch.

There's still another ten minutes before my break is over, but I also don't want to sit here with all my conversational skills coming to a halt. It'd be easier if I knew how to react around him.

"I'm gonna," I hike my thumb over my shoulder, "get back to work. My break is almost up and I probably need to save the new guys from whatever else the night is going to bring."

Eyes narrowed, he nods. "I'll catch you later, then."

I hurry out of my seat almost knocking the chair over. It's like he knows I was lying about my break being over. I'm pretty sure he does, and he's not happy about it. It was the only thing I could think of to get me out of his presence as fast as possible.

The rest of the night goes by without a hitch. People finally stopped coming in, and we begin our clean up routine. I'm wiping down the counter when I look up. Cami and Derrick are huddled close together, whispering.

I'm not exactly sure how I feel about that. When did they become all buddy-buddy? My only guess is they became friends over the summer when she'd hang out with Travis. I politely refused those invitations because I knew he would be there. And...I didn't know then what I know now.

Cami and I are finally home after a long night at work. I can hear my bed calling my name. Beckoning me toward the fluffy pillow and sleep. But, I need to talk to Cami first.

"So," I begin. "You and Derrick sure seemed cozy earlier?" Crap, that came off super jealous, and not at all the way I meant it. I'd be lying if I said there wasn't a twinge of irritation at how easily they talked to each other.

"Are you jealous, Darcy?"

"Not at all. I just didn't know y'all were such close friends." I rush the words out of my mouth. Trying to play it cool and failing.

She rolls her eyes, seeing through my weak bravado. "You have nothing to worry about, girl. You know Travis is the only person I care about."

"I know that," I whine. "I'm just curious."

"Didn't anyone ever tell you curiosity killed the cat?"

I laugh. She's right, but that doesn't stop the wondering. Doesn't stop the hope that maybe they were discussing me. Ugh, I'm such a mess. I've never been this conflicted in my life.

"Fine," she sighs as if I'm torturing her or something. "If you must know, he was asking me if I knew anything about the basketball players or coaches. He was trying to get a little intel to help better his chances at making the team."

"Oh." My shoulders sag. I walk backward until the backs of my knees hit the edge of the bed before sitting down. Sadness hits me with a pang. The reality that he's actually set on us being *just* friends hits me hard.

Frustration sweeps through my veins shortly after that. I have no right to be upset. I'm the one that suggested we be friends. This is my own doing. I could have taken the chance to see where things might have gone when he came over here yesterday. Instead, I took the coward's way out insisting on keeping things platonic.

"Are you okay?" Cami crosses the room and squats down in front of me. Her eyebrows furrowed, and a pinched smile on her face, clearly concerned.

Shaking myself from my inner turmoil, I reply, "Yeah, I'm fine. I hope you can help him out. He's wanted to play for a long time. It would mean everything to him."

If my voice catches on that last sentence it's not my fault. I used to mean everything to him. Another sting of frustration hits me.

"I hung out with a few of the players back when I used to party all the time. I'll put in a good word for him." She winks and goes back to her side of the room.

I go to the bathroom everyone on this floor shares and brush my teeth. Cami is on the phone with Travis when I come back into the room.

I quickly change into my pajamas and put my hair into a messy bun. Climbing under the sheets, I grab the headphones from my nightstand and connect them to my phone. I scroll through Spotify until I find the most woe is me playlist possible and press play.

As music softly plays through the speakers, drowning out Cami's conversation, I replay my interactions with Derrick today. I definitely could have handled that better. Learning to be comfortable around him is going to be hard, but I'll have to figure something out. A tear streams down my face as acceptance that I have no chance with him begins to sink in.

derrick

THERE ARE days when Cami drives me up the wall, and others where I'm happy she is on my side, willing to help in my crazy endeavors. This is one of those days that I'm happy my best friend chose an awesome girlfriend.

Cami and I had a quick discussion at Roasted the other night about an idea I had. Today...we're hatching a plan for Labor Day weekend. One that will no doubt have Darcy back in my arms as more than a friend. But, it has to start out as a friends' type of trip so she doesn't become suspicious.

I'm sitting in the chair by the desk, swiveling back and forth. A small part of it is excitement over what this scheme could mean, a large part because I'm a huge fucking kid.

"She definitely still has feelings for you," Cami says. She's lying on Travis's bed flipping through a magazine she brought along with her.

"How do you know that?"

She rolls her eyes. She does that a lot in my presence. Am I *that* dense? "Because she all but interrogated me when we got home. For a minute I thought she was going to shake me until I gave her some answers."

I frown, rubbing the back of my neck. "Why would she question you?" I honestly don't know why Darcy would ask Cami about me. Hell, she couldn't even stand to be in my vicinity for five minutes. Or, maybe she didn't know how to act? Her behavior the other day was odd all the way around.

"Because, dummy," she sighs, exasperated. "She saw us talking and she wanted to know what we were talking about." She lifts a hand from the page she's currently reading and taps her chin. "She was definitely jealous. At least, that's the vibe she gave off."

"Y'all are ridiculous," Travis says from the top of the bed. His head is buried in a textbook, pen scratching in the notebook he has on the other side of him. I should get him one of those little lap desk things I see kids use. If only so he doesn't look so damn uncomfortable when he's studying.

"What?" I ask. Sarcasm dripping from my mouth. "I'm no such thing. I'm optimistic." I turn back to Cami. "So, what did you tell her? Not the truth, I hope."

"I'm not a moron." She grabs one of the decorative pillows she bought to brighten the place up and throws it at my head. It hits me square in the face. Damn, she should play sports. The girl's got an arm, and it kind of hurt.

"What did you tell her we were talking about?"

"Basketball, duh. It's pretty much the only thing you focus on other than Darcy."

I jerk my head back. "Why in the hell would I ask you about basketball?"

Shrugging, she goes back to her magazine. "Eh, I told her that you asked if I knew any of the basketball players. And that I would put in a good word for you with them."

"I'm still lost."

"It wasn't a far-fetched reason for us to be talking. I did, in fact, used to hang out with the players while I was partying hard. But, I will at least tell them to check you out so I'm not a complete liar."

"You are a fucking genius." I'm so happy she was able to come up with something on the spot that I want to scoop her up and twirl her around. Travis probably wouldn't be a fan of that, so I lean back in my chair and cross my arms. "So, she was jealous, huh?"

"Totally," Cami snorts. "She may *say* she just wants to be friends, but that's definitely not the case. After I told her, she deflated."

"What do you mean?"

"I mean, she looked really sad. Like I took a pin and popped her bubble of hope." She's silent for a few moments. I can practically see the gears turning in her brain. "I think she's wanting you to pursue her. Darcy wants to know that you're serious and still want her."

"That's what I've been trying to do," I raise my voice in frustration, almost growling. "She keeps blocking me at every attempt. And...when I try to make small talk with her, she clams up and makes bullshit excuses about her break being over when I know it hadn't been fifteen minutes."

"Or she runs," Travis adds.

"Thanks for the reminder, douchebag." I grab the pillow Cami threw at me and lob it at him. It doesn't hit him in the face, but it knocks the textbook out of his hand. When he narrows his eyes at me, I feel a small thrill of satisfaction course through me. His annoyance shouldn't make me happy, but I'm frustrated that nothing I try seems to be working. So, yes, getting a reaction out of him amuses me.

"Aren't y'all supposed to be discussing what you're going to do with this little pow-wow here?" He sweeps his hand from me to Cami. "I still want no part of it, but I can't even take my girl to dinner because y'all have *planning* to do." He uses annoying little air quotes when he says planning.

"Yep," Cami sits up and scoots closer to Travis. "And, I have the perfect plan."

"I'm not going to like it, am I?" Travis groans.

"Probably not," she chirps. "But you'll do it anyway because you love me and have no choice."

She lays out the plan, and it's solid. It'll be a way for all of us to hang out without me being pushy about a relationship status. The whole thing will be completely organic. Now, I just have to hope Darcy doesn't shoot it down.

* * *

Operation win Darcy back is just days away and I am starting to get nervous. Cami must not have said anything to her yet because she isn't acting any different. I only hope that this plan goes off without a hitch.

We will go on our little adventure in a week, but I realized pretty soon after we planned this that I don't have any equipment for this trip. I also never realized how many people visit a sports and outdoor store. This place is crowded, which I guess is normal, if they had the same idea that we have for Labor Day weekend. Families bustle up and down the aisle grabbing gear off shelves and placing them in their basket.

I stare at the headers of the aisles trying to figure out where everything I need is. I've never been on a trip like this before so I had to go online and print off a checklist just to make sure I have everything to make it successful. Hope bubbled up inside me at what this could mean for my relationship with Darcy.

An employee comes from behind and taps me on the shoulder, "Is there anything I can help you with?" Her voice is sugary sweet and full of kindness.

"Actually, yes," I blush while playing with the edges of the paper in my hand. And, I'm not blushing because I find her attractive or anything, but because I feel like a complete dumbass for not knowing where to find the stuff. "Could you tell me where these things are?"

She holds her hand out, waiting for me to place the paper in her hand. "Sure," she looks over the list. "You can find all of these items between aisles seventeen and twenty-one."

"Thanks," I mumble, embarrassed.

"No problem," she chirps before she turns around to help another customer.

Directing my cart toward the aisles she pointed me to, I dodge and weave between other people trying to get their items. I've never been in this area of a sports store. I typically go where the basketballs and athletic clothes are, grab what I need and leave. But, apparently there are a slew of people who really enjoy the outdoors.

I find the section that holds the tents and have no clue which one to get. The options are endless, varying from a tiny one-person tent to one that looks like it could hold a family of eight. I would get the one-person tent but I don't want to give her the idea that I'm only after one thing. Even though, I want her as close to me as possible.

In the end, I decided on a two-person tent that has a section in the middle that can be zipped up. Darcy will at least have some sense of privacy with this option. I grab two because I highly doubt that Travis owns a tent. Next up on the list are chairs. As much as I would rather spend time with Darcy alone in the tent, we're going to need a place to sit, obviously.

Finally, I'm in the ridiculously long checkout line, not quite so patiently waiting for my turn. When the associate finishes ringing up my items, I almost blanch at the total before I insert my credit card into the little slot and confirm the purchase. Mom and dad are going to freak out whenever they see the bill. But, I'm going to be honest with them about the purchase and hope they will be completely understanding. Hell, they will probably jump for joy because they loved Darcy. Mom was just as upset as I was when Darcy stopped speaking to me. She was just so happy that her son found someone who might settle him down a little bit. If only she knew how right she was. Darcy makes me feel grounded.

The walk to the car is just as hazardous as it was walking around the store. Cars are zipping in and out of parking spots. Some people are driving like a bat out of hell trying to find parking. I only want to get to Travis's SUV without being run over.

All the new gear is loaded in the back. As I shut the hatch, I wonder where the hell we are going to store it all. Our dorm room is a nice size, but it's not massive or anything. My mind drifts to Darcy. What if she doesn't come on this trip with us. I hope Cami works her magic because everything hangs on her convincing Darcy to tag along.

darcy

"NO, NO WAY," I am mere decibels from yelling. "I'm not going on this trip with you. Have you lost your mind?"

That's the only thing I can think when Cami describes the camping trip she wants us all to go on this weekend. It's Labor Day weekend, the first long-ish break from classes. I plan on reading some comic books, watching a few movies, and just relaxing. My plan does *not* include roughing it with Cami, Travis, and Derrick.

"Why not?" Cami asks, completely serious. Like it's totally unreasonable for me to not want to go with them.

"For starts," I tick off a finger on my hand as if it's a list. "There's work."

Before I have a chance to continue with the reasons I can't go, Cami begins speaking. "Already taken care of. I asked Tom if we could both take off since the shop is pretty much dead on holiday weekends."

I stare at her in stunned silence. The only thing that can be heard is Post Malone talking about being a rock star through Cami's portable speaker.

"You did what?" I'm certain I didn't hear her correctly. There's no way in hell she would be that presumptuous.

"I talked to Tom," she runs her fingers through her dark hair, separating it into sections before she begins braiding it. "He agreed as soon as the words left my mouth. He said you deserve a break to have fun and loosen up some."

My mouth hangs open. I'm shocked. That's putting it mildly, actually. I'm borderline pissed. How dare she talk to Tom about my schedule. And, what the hell is Tom thinking telling her I need to relax. It's honestly none of their business how I choose to spend my time. I like order, and I happen to enjoy the pace at which I live my life. Things tend to become stressful sometimes, sure. But, I put that pressure on myself so I can be the absolute best version of myself.

"I'm not even going to comment on the stunt you pulled to get me off work. Just know that I'm not happy about it." My fists are curled into balls at my side. Fingernails digging small crescents into the skin. "But Derrick is the other problem."

"I thought you two were friends, now," Cami sighs. She acts like I'm some petulant child that needs things explained to me in small words.

"We are," I stammer. "But that doesn't mean I want

to spend a four-day weekend with him." A small voice inside my head calls me a liar. I quickly shut that voice up. Truth or not, it's not a good idea for either of us. He's focused on basketball, and I'm focused on school. There's not time for anything else.

"Well, friends hang out," Cami argues. "I mean, I never would have gotten close to Travis had I not gone on that *friend* date with him."

She has a point, but I'm not going to tell her that. My situation is also a tad bit different. Derrick and I have a history. Ugh, when did I become such a drama queen? The old Darcy would have gone with the flow. But the new Darcy? The new Darcy is terrified of letting her walls down around Derrick. Even if I secretly want to let my guard drop completely.

"Okay," I drawl. "But I haven't been camping in years. I'm not sure I even like it anymore."

"This is a great way to find out." Cami puts an elastic band at the end of the braid she's just finished. "You've told me tons of stories about how much fun you had camping with your family as a kid."

It's true. Some of my best memories are of me, my brother, and cousins fishing, exploring, and telling each other spooky stories by the campfire. We had a blast, and they are moments I will always cherish. They were happy, simple times when I didn't have a care in the world.

Cami continues, "Besides, you have to come. None of us have been camping before and need you there to show us the ropes. We may never make it back alive if you aren't around."

"That's a bit much, don't you think?" I laugh. "I'm sure you will be perfectly fine without me."

Cami pokes her bottom lip out and widening her eyes, pouting. She's crazy if she thinks this sad puppy look is going to wear me down. "Do it for me? You wouldn't leave me surrounded by two guys who will probably get us lost before we even get to the campsite, would you?"

Gah, she's absolutely ridiculous sometimes, but I wouldn't have her any other way. I stay quiet for a moment, letting her sweat it out. She keeps exaggerating her pout and I can't stop the giggle falling from my lips. "Fine, I'll think about it."

"Well you better think fast. We leave tomorrow afternoon." With that said, she picks up a textbook, and begins studying. Like she didn't just ruin all of my plans for the weekend.

A shirt sails by my face as Cami tries to find clothes to pack for the camping trip. The room is a mess. Piles of clothes litter the floor and the destruction is making me twitchy. I'm not really sure what Cami is expecting out of this trip. I mean, it's not a fashion runway show. If anything, it's the one time to get away with wearing T-shirts and yoga pants or shorts.

"I have absolutely nothing to wear," Cami whines. "What the hell do you even pack for trip like this?"

I study the chaos surrounding me before looking back at Cami. "Definitely not any of this. Comfortable is the key to camping."

A small duffel bag sits on my bed, empty. Yes, I decided to go on this adventure against my better judgment. I just hope it doesn't come back to bite me in the ass.

"Girl, you better start packing we leave in an hour."

"There isn't much I really need to take. The more you pack the more you have to keep up with, and I've lost many of flip-flops to the vast debt of the lake."

I walk to my dresser and pull open the first drawer. Everything is lined up in neat tidy rows making it easier for me to find what I need. We will be gone for three nights and three days, and I calculate how many of each thing I will need. I grab enough underwear and sports bras for the exact amount of days we will be gone but decide to grab a few more because things like getting thrown into the lake tend to happen. Being prepared is one of the things that I pride myself on, and let's face it, nobody likes to be walking around wet all day unless they're actually in the lake.

Before closing the drawer, I also pick up a few camisoles. They make great cover ups for bathing suits. Crap, I forgot I am going to need to wear a bathing suit and the only one that I have will make it overly apparent that I am a geek at heart.

After throwing the items in my hand on the bed I turn toward the small closet that Cami and I share. Her side is a hot mess. Clothes drooping off the hangers in disarray, and there is absolutely no order to any of it. My side of the closet, on the other hand, shows a level of stability. My shirts are color-coded, and everything is in order from tank tops to long sleeve so I can easily find something to wear depending on the weather.

However, there is a box hidden behind my shoes containing all of my geeky glory. And, that is where I find my Wonder Woman bathing suit. There are a few others in there as well, but I'm not even sure if they still fit.

I don't realize that Cami is hovering over me until I hear a small gasp. "Is that your box of shame?"

I snort, "Hardly. This is the one box of old Darcy that I allowed myself to bring from home."

She bends down, takes the box out of my hands, and walks out of the closet. Where the hell does she think she's taking my stuff? I peek around the closet door. She's sitting on my bed, pulling out every piece of clothing the box contains. I can hear her laugh and can only imagine that she's made it to the bottom where all my superhero figurines lie.

"You weren't kidding when you said that you were a geek. You are basically the queen of geekdom." She sees the horror stricken look on my face, and rushes on. "There isn't anything wrong with that, you know?"

Sighing, I walk out of the closet and sit down next to

her. "I know. I just felt like I needed to reinvent myself when I got to college."

"Girl," Cami puts her arm around my shoulders. "You don't need to impress anyone. Be who you are. If anyone changes their mind about how they see you, that's their problem. Not yours." She picks up one of my tank tops that says "Talk Nerdy to Me" and grins. "You should only take these clothes with you this weekend. Throw caution the wind and live a little."

Just the thought of pushing aside my new orderly tendencies sends a chill through me. I can't tell if it's fear, or excitement, but decide that maybe Cami is right. Maybe I need to do what she says. She opened up to my suggestions last year, it's only fair that I do the same right now. This could be the beginning of finding myself again.

I grab the tank tops, shirts, and bathing suits and throw them in the bag haphazardly. All I really need now is my toiletries and shorts. I dig through another drawer until I find a few pairs of soft shorts and jean shorts, throwing them on top of the other clothes.

Cami is frantically going around her side of the room, digging through the clothes on the floor until she finds enough clothes to stuff into her backpack. While she's running around like a crazy person, I pull two ziplock bags from my desk. I keep them for snacks I don't finish, and to store pretty much anything and everything.

I throw one in Cami's direction, and she looks at it

with a pinched face, obviously confused. "It's for your toothbrush and stuff."

"Okay, so maybe don't lose all your planning abilities." She shoves her toothbrush and toothpaste into the bag. "You seriously think of everything, and I would have had a toothpaste mess all over my clothes if it wasn't for you."

"I don't plan on losing the preparedness. I mean, who would take care of you if the beginnings of a zombie apocalypse broke out?"

"First, I don't think I've ever heard you mention zombie anything. Clearly, your inner geek is already coming out in full force, and I happen to love it." She zips up her backpack, setting it on the edge of the bed and eyes the mess she's made. "Second, I would hope that maybe Travis could take care of me, but I'm pretty sure I'd be better off with you around."

"Duh," I roll my eyes. "Nothing against Travis, but he hasn't spent his life reading zombie comics, books, or watching The Walking Dead. I know I'm the better option when it comes to surviving. At least, when the recently deceased are around."

"You are so weird," she laughs.

"Hey, you wanted me to let my inner geek out. This isn't even the half of it."

"The guys should be here soon." She glances at the mess she made, again. I can practically see the debate she's have with herself over what she should do. "I guess I should clean some of this up?"

She says it as a question, hoping that I'll let it slide. But she should know me better than that. "Please... Looking at it is about to give me an eye twitch."

"Too bad you don't have the same policy of clothes on the floor as I do. Because if you were me, you'd leave and hope it disappears by the time we get back."

"Alas," I shake my head. "I'm not you, and we'll have an even bigger mess when we get back from camping. It's probably best to get it done now."

"I guess you're right." She begins picking up clothes and throwing them on her bed. I feel bad having her do it on her own, so I walk over and start folding everything. Even if it's not put up before we leave, at least they are off the floor.

Cami stands next to me, picking up a shirt, folding it, and placing it next to the stack I've already started. She bumps my hip with her own. "You know everything is going to be okay, right?"

My eyebrow arches. "What do you mean?"

"With Derrick. I'm glad y'all are trying to be friends." She bends down until her eyes meet mine. "But, even if y'all take things past that... It will be alright. I'm here for you no matter what. I just want you to know that."

"Thanks," I whisper. Now, I'm really freaking out about how this weekend is going to go. I know she means well, but I'm starting to have second thoughts about whether I should even go.

The choice is taken out of my hands when there is a

knock on the door. Cami doesn't hesitate yelling, "Come in."

I laugh. Not that long ago we were trying to find the closest weapon available when Derrick was at the door. It's different, I know, since we are expecting their arrival. But it's still funny. Maybe I'll get Cami an aluminum bat for her birthday so we at least have something if we ever need it.

Travis opens the door, and sticks his head in. "Are y'all decent in here?"

"Kind of late to ask that," Cami says pulling the door open wider and jumping into his arms.

They are annoyingly sweet together, and I'm happy that Cami found her person. The one she can be herself around and not have to worry about added pressure.

"Hi," Derrick says from behind Travis.

"Hi." I give a small wave. I can't stop the butterflies from erupting in my stomach. Hell, I'm pretty sure they are doing somersaults.

"Are y'all ready to go?" Travis asks over Cami's head.

"Yep," I reply.

I start to grab the bag off of my bed, but Derrick beats me to it. "A lady should never carry her own bags."

My cheeks redden. "Um, thanks."

As soon as everyone is out of the room, I close the door and lock it. We make our way to Travis's SUV, and they try to find space to put our bags. The back is full to the brim with camping gear. It looks like someone bought the entire outdoor section. I guess whoever bought everything wanted to be prepared for any situation.

Cami climbs into the front seat next to Travis, which leaves Derrick and I in the back seat. I look in the space between us and see a pile of my favorite snacks. Hot fries, M&M's, and Big Red. I look up at Derrick.

He rubs the back of his neck, suddenly nervous. "We stopped at a store before coming over here. I grabbed these because it's what you used to always have with you when..." He trails off, not finishing the sentence.

But he doesn't have to. "We were together" hangs in the air. I smile, "Thank you."

He just nods and opens his bag of Twizzlers. Maybe this trip won't be so bad after all. I sneak a glance at Derrick. Our eyes meet and he diverts his attention. Yep, the butterflies are definitely back in full force.

derrick

THE DRIVE to Colorado Bend Lake shouldn't take long. It is only about an hour away from Austin, plus another 30 minutes from Hilltop. I'm beginning to get antsy because I don't know what to do right now.

The way Darcy looked at me when she saw the snacks I had lined up on the seat let me know that the surprise was appreciated. Not sure what to talk about, I stare at the window taking in the scenery. Cami, for some ungodly reason, has control of the radio. A song by In This Moment blares through the speakers and Cami is singing along at the top of her lungs.

I look out of the corner of my eye to gauge Darcy's reaction to her best friend. Her hand is covering her mouth trying to hold back laughter, and the twinkle in her eye shows just how amused she is at her best friend's crazy singing. I'm not even sure how these two became best friends, but I guess close proximity will do that, eventually.

They make such an unlikely pair. Cami is loud, boisterous, and unafraid to be herself. On the other hand, Darcy is shy, quiet, thinks before she speaks, and almost seems unsure of herself. The Darcy I used to know, while still quiet and shy, knew who she was. I'm trying to reconcile that Darcy with the one sitting across the seat from me. Hopefully, pieces of the girl I used to know shine through over the weekend.

The car begins to slow, much earlier than we should be, as we take a right onto the exit ramp before pulling into a gas station and coming to a complete stop.

"Why are we here?" I ask as Cami quickly pushes the door open and rushes out.

Travis turns down the radio so that he doesn't have to yell to answer me. "She had to go to the restroom. Does anyone need anything while I go inside?"

Darcy and I both shake our heads no. I honestly can't believe that Cami already has to pee. We've only been on the road for a little over thirty minutes. The stop so quickly in the beginning of our trip makes me leery of taking any longer trips with Travis and Cami in the future.

"So, is this normal for her?" I turn my body toward Darcy waiting for her response.

She doesn't answer right away, instead she studies our surroundings. The gas station doesn't look like it sees a lot of visitors. The sign is faded so much you can barely read it, and the building looks as if it could use a fresh coat of paint. Now I'm curious what the inside might look like, but I don't really feel like investigating that.

That is how scary movies start out. A bunch of dumb, innocent teenagers stop at a decrepit gas station because someone has to pee, and then BAM, they all die.

Finally, she acknowledges my question, pulling me out of my horror filled imagination. "Honestly, yeah. I don't even think my cousin's kids go to the restroom as much as Cami does. And they are two and four years old."

"Wow," I exclaim in shock. "How do she and Travis even get through an actual date?"

Darcy shrugs, "I have no idea. The only time I've been around them is on their very first 'friend' date, and she spent most of that time glaring at him." I like how she used finger quotes around *friend*.

I chuckle remembering the conversation I had with Travis before he took her on that date. I was worried Cami was going to break his heart. I wasn't entirely sure that things were going to go well with them when he explained just how much she loathed him. But I did my duty as best friend. I gave him some advice and let him know I would be there for him if he needed it.

Darcy's eyebrows pinch in confusion. "What's so funny?"

"Nothing. I just remember Travis telling me about

that day, and how he scored an actual date with her by beating her at bowling."

Darcy starts to laugh. "That was pretty genius of him, actually. You should've seen the look on Cami's face whenever he rolled the last bowling ball down the lane."

"I really wish I could've been there to see that."

Just as I'm about to ask if she's okay with this trip, Cami opens the door and studies our amused expressions. "What are you two laughing about?"

"Nothing," we both shout at the same time and burst into another fit of laughter.

Cami rolls her eyes and slides into her seat before turning the volume of the radio back up. Moments later Travis gets into the car and we are back on the road. The rest of the trip should be smooth sailing as long as Cami doesn't have to take anymore potty breaks.

Darcy's hand brushes mine as she reaches for her bag of hot fries. I'm not sure if it was intentional or not, but the pang of longing I feel is sharp and hits me hard. I lean back and try to get comfortable. Stretching my legs as much as I can with Travis sitting in front me. My eyes close against the harsh sunlight beating through the window, and I try to doze off with Cami's racket playing in the background.

The car comes to a stop and my eyes pop open. I'm really hoping that means we're at the campsite, but you never really know with Cami in the car. We had to stop *again* so that she could go to bathroom. I swear, she has the bladder of an excited puppy.

I'm not disappointed when I see an expanse of cleared out space, dotted with tents, and the lake just beyond that. It's serene out here, and I'm glad Cami suggested it. She got the idea after a day trip Travis took her on when he was trying to win her over.

I look over at Darcy. Her eyes are wide and excitement sparkles through them. I've never been camping before so I'm not sure what to expect. But, I'm hoping Darcy leads the way with all her know how on pretty much everything.

The lake is calm and inviting, beckoning me to jump in right this very moment. And I'm tempted...so tempted to do just that. But, I hear the back hatch open and Darcy is already pulling items out. My shoulders slump. The lake will have to wait. I can almost hear the whimpers from the water as I round the car and help Darcy.

The tents are piled in our allotted camping area. The ice chests and chairs thrown haphazardly around them. Everything else is still in the car until we get the tents set up. I stand for a moment taking in the area around us. Other tents are set up a decent distance from us to give us a bit of privacy. But down the narrow road, huge campers are lined up resembling a small city of travelers.

"Why can't we camp like they are?" I don't ask anyone in particular, and I'm not expecting an answer. But one comes anyway.

"Because none of us own a camper, or a way to pull it, Genius." I definitely don't miss the sarcasm pouring off of Travis. I don't know why he's being an ass. He needs to cheer up because this whole weekend is supposed to be spent wooing Darcy.

Not bothering with a response, I pull the first tent out of its bag. Rods and fabric fall into a heap on the ground. What? I thought it was going to be like those emergency rafts. You pull a string and it pops up already assembled. Clearly, I am out of my element. How does one put a tent together?

A sheet of paper lying next to one of the rods pulls my attention to it. I guess they can be called instructions, but really, it's just a paper with diagrams and arrows. It reminds me of the "instructions" that Ikea items come with, and I'm dreading the amount of work it's likely going to take.

Pulling out my phone, I begin entering the brand name of the tent into the search bar. Maybe I can save some time and find a video tutorial. When I hit search, the faded little circle spins around and around. Of course, no service. Did Cami even check phone reception for this place before she picked it?

Darcy bends down to start assembling the tent, but I stop her with a hand on her shoulder. "I can do it, go hang out with Cami."

She gives me an impervious grin. "Are you sure you can handle it? You looked scared when you pulled it out of the bag."

"I'll have you know, I am perfectly capable of putting this contraption together."

"Have at it, caveman." She rolls her eyes, nods toward Cami, and they walk off together.

"Where are you going?" I call to their retreating backs.

"To the bathroom," Darcy hollers back. "Unless, of course, you need my help."

"Carry on," I reply.

Her laughter drifts through the air, and I shake my head. That girl is something else. Now, I need to prove her wrong and show her that I can, in fact, put this tent together.

* * *

The tent assembly did not go well at all. After a few tries, and damn near throwing the thing into the lake, I asked the campers in the lot next to us to help me. They are an older couple, and choose a different campsite to visit every Labor Day weekend. I'm more than grateful that they chose this lake. Without Mr. Campbell's help, we'd be sleeping on the rock-hard ground.

Travis was exactly zero help. As soon as the girls got back from the restroom, he joined them by the water, arm slung over Cami's shoulders. All while I, and Mr. Campbell, got these things set up and ready for us. I swear, they should teach this in high school, or something. The class could be called "Trying to win a girl with a camping trip? Here's how you set up a fucking tent." That course would have been extremely helpful.

The sun is dipping low on the horizon, bringing in a starry night sky. All of our bags are placed inside the tents, courtesy of Travis. He did help with one thing. The ice chests are open waiting for us to fix our dinner.

Travis and I decided to keep it simple tonight with dinner. We assumed, correctly might I add, that we wouldn't have much time to make something elaborate. There's a grocery store about five miles from the campgrounds entrance that we will visit first thing in the morning. Tonight, we shall dine on a feast of sandwiches.

"The tents look good, Derrick." Darcy is smothering her slice of bread with Miracle Whip. I knew there was something odd about her. Oh well, it doesn't change how I feel about her in the slightest. Even if she does have horrible taste in condiments.

"Oh, um," I look everywhere except for at her. "Thanks?" It comes out as a question instead of a statement. Honestly, I don't deserve all the praise. She would be singing a different tune if it weren't for our friendly neighbors.

"It's okay," she whispers in my ear. "I know you had help. But I'm proud of you for asking for the help, rather than making a huge mess of things."

First off, how did she sneak up on me so quietly. Second, I can't stop the heat rising to my cheeks. I don't think I've ever blushed in my life. But having her here...

this close…makes me want to turn my head and kiss her. I don't because I'm a gentleman. The urge is there, though.

We eat in almost silence. The exception being Cami, who is talking at a speed I didn't know was possible, about God knows what. I've learned to tune her out for the most part.

"I don't know about y'all, but I'm ready for bed." Darcy announces.

"Already?" Cami whines.

"Yep. I spent the day trying to get all my homework done so I'm not scrambling to finish it Monday night."

"This is why you are the smart one." Cami bats her eyelashes.

"Flattery will get you everywhere, Darling," Darcy says as if she's an actress from those old black and white films my parents watch. "Now, which tent is ours?"

Cami looks like a deer caught in headlights. "Ummmmm."

Travis chuckles, amused with the question. He knows damn well I intended to share my tent with Darcy. But he also knows this is about to get complicated. Dammit. I should have seen this coming.

"Well," Cami begins. "I was going to stay in the same tent as Travis."

"And leave me to share with Derrick?" Darcy shrieks.

"Am I that horrible of a roomie option?" Mock hurt lacing my words. Okay, so maybe there is a bit of real disappointment. But I should have known better.

Darcy looks like she's about to freak out. She may have been easy going all day long, but this situation makes her uncomfortable. I don't want to be the guy that makes her feel this way.

"I have a suggestion," I say. Travis groans. He knows exactly where I'm going with this. "You and Cami can take one of the tents, and Travis and I will share the other." If looks could kill, I would be a blob on the ground with the glare Travis is directing my way.

"Are you sure?" Darcy's voice is quiet. "I don't want to put them out."

"Yes," I sigh. "I'm sure. We can revisit the sleeping situation tomorrow. Work out some sort of arrangement that still gives Travis and Cami some *alone* time."

Cami is pouting. She'll have to get over it. I will do anything to put a smile on Darcy's face. Even if that means bunking with the person I see every damn day.

"Okay." She makes her way to the tent that has both of our things. I follow so that I can grab my bag and put it in the tent on the other side of the campfire.

"Thank you," she whispers before zipping the entrance closed.

I can already hear the arguments Travis is going to make when we turn in for the night. But it doesn't matter. Tomorrow will be interesting. I'll have to do everything in my power to make sure she feels safe enough to share a tent with me.

darcy

CRICKETS CHIRP softly in the night. The darkness engulfing them while they sing their nightly tune. Cami snores softly on the other side of the partition in our tent.

I shouldn't even be awake since I was the one who claimed sleepiness to avoid Derrick. The playful banter and jokes were fun, but I needed to take a step back. I'm not even sure why I whispered in his ear. It felt amazing at the time to shake him up and give him a little taste of what I feel with his shameless flirting. But now, I'm regretting giving him any sort of false hope when it comes to me.

As if that's not enough, I also feel a tremendous amount of guilt. I didn't mean to steal Cami away from Travis, but I did all the same. I just assumed that the sleeping arrangements would be just like in the dorms, Travis and Derrick in one tent and Cami and I in the other. I feel like a moron for even assuming that. Of course, Cami and Travis would want time for themselves, and want a little bit of privacy. This is a sort of mini vacation for them. Away from the pressures of school, and Mr. Burgess's knowing eyes. That was Cami's biggest complaint when she got back to school. Tonya's dad was always keeping an eye on her, doing his best to keep her on the straight and narrow. I'm happy she has some sort of parental support, even if it's not from her own.

Tomorrow I plan on doing everything in my power to make it up to the both of them. Even if that means bunking with Derrick for the next two nights. I can only hope that the both of us are on the same wavelength and don't expect more than friendship. That thought alone sends a pang of sadness straight to my heart. As much as I want to be more than friends, I'm not sure that he would be a fan of new Darcy, no matter what he says. It's also not a good idea. Not with my course, or work, load.

At the rate my thoughts are bouncing around in my head, sleep will not come easily. I do my best to help it along, close eyes, and let the symphony of the night lull me to slumber.

* * *

Shockingly, Cami is the one to wake *me* up. It's such a rare occurrence that I think I'm dreaming for a second.

Usually, I'm the one that has to almost physically pulled her from her bed each morning.

"Why are you awake?" I asked rubbing the sleep from my eyes. "You do realize we are on vacation, don't you?"

"I need to pee, really bad," she whispers screeches. "And I swear on all things holy something brushed against my leg."

Lifting my head up I see a small gap in the tent door and roll my eyes. "You didn't close the tent all the way. I'm sure it was just a bug or something."

"Bug, or not, something freaking touched me and I need out of this tent now." She scurries out from under her sleeping bag, almost tripping when her foot is caught in the opening. "I knew I should have thought of something else for this trip," she mumbles. I try to cover the laugh bubbling up, but it doesn't work. She stops long enough to glare at me before stomping out of the tent. I wonder what she meant by that last comment, or if I was even supposed to hear it.

I lie back down and pull a pillow over my face, attempting to fall back into the very yummy dream I was having about a certain hammer wielding superhero.

Not even five minutes have passed before Derrick pokes his head inside the tent. "Are you up?"

"No," I deadpan, groaning. "What is wrong with you people? Any other day y'all sleep until *noon*." I throw my pillow to the side and sit up. "Now, all of a sudden, you're early birds who rise with the freaking sun."

He chuckles. He's *effing* laughing at me. "What is so funny?"

"You," he's still laughing, but trying to get it under control. "I don't think I've seen you this riled up since you saw me at the coffee shop."

"Ugh." I'm not seeing the humor in this situation at all. "You are just as infuriating now as you were then. Can I please go back to sleep? I don't get to do this whole sleeping in thing very often."

"No dice, sleepyhead." He opens the tent wider.

The sunshine pours in making me squint my eyes against the brightness. "Why not?"

"Because Travis is starving and Cami keeps looking at the tent like it attacked her."

"A little bug crawling on her does not deserve that type of reaction." She's making it really hard to make things up to her and Travis today. Confusion is written all over Derrick's face, so I continue. "She didn't close the tent all the way, a creepy crawly made its way in, and touched her. She's freaking out about nothing."

Now he's laughing, uncontrollably. Holding his stomach as he doubles over. I wouldn't be surprised if he has tears running down his cheeks by how hard he's laughing.

"It's really not that funny."

"Oh, but it is," he gasps. "Though, it's not surprising. She's not really the outdoorsy type."

I throw the blankets off of me, sit up, and stretch my arms over my head. The soreness of sleeping on the ground is definitely not something I missed. I don't remember it being this horrible when I was kid.

Derrick isn't laughing anymore. When I look up, his eyes are trailing my body. His gaze begins at my now bare legs before traveling to the sliver of stomach showing from my arms being raised. Finally, his eyes rest on mine. I see so much behind those eyes. Desire. Confusion. Lust.

He clears his throat. "We should probably feed the crazies before they turn to cannibalism."

Without waiting for a reply, he turns around and walks off. But, he looks back and I'd be lying if I said I didn't like the way he's looking at me.

* * *

The ride to the grocery store is tense. Almost all of us are wearing scowls on our faces as if they are party accessories. And I say almost because the only one still smiling is Derrick.

I feel as if I'm the only one who has a perfectly good reason to be in a bad mood. Both Cami and Travis are known for being night owls and not waking up until after lunch the next day, but this morning is their own doing. So, they shouldn't get to wear angry faces. And maybe, just maybe, this could've been avoided if they would've been a little more prepared and packed pop tarts or something for us to eat before going to the grocery store. Had they told me about this trip more than a day before we were leaving I would have happily let them know everything we were going to need.

The only thing I can't figure out is why Derrick is in such a good mood. He's usually in the same boat as Cami and Travis, but a small part of me hopes that I could be the reason. The other part of me wants to slap me and tell me I need to be thinking straight. I swear, I'm walking around with an angel and devil on either shoulder, and I have no clue which one I should listen to.

The grocery store, we're pulling up to, reminds me of that rundown gas station we stopped at yesterday. Who knows if the food in this place is even fresh. I kind of want to stay in the car while they go get food drinks and supplies for the rest of the weekend. The thought of leaving those three in charge of getting stuff sends a shiver down my spine. If I don't go in there with them, we will be back at the store again tomorrow. That fact alone is what has me pulling the latch on the car door as soon as it comes to a stop.

The door to the store is glass but dingy, and you can barely see through it. That is definitely not building up my confidence that we will find what we need here, but I open the door anyway.

I'm shocked to find a well-lit store and aisles of food ready for our browsing pleasure. Obviously, I was a little judgmental before we came inside. In my defense, they should really keep up the outside appearances on this place if they don't want to freak people out. I wonder if they have one those little suggestion boxes some places have. I could leave a tiny piece of constructive criticism. I'm actually a little surprised it looks the way it does since it's so close to the lake. It's definitely not inviting.

Cami and Travis take off in one direction leaving me with Derrick. I feel like I should be doing *something* and grab a cart. If for nothing else than to have something to do with my hands. It's better that they're on the cart handle than hanging awkwardly at my sides.

"Are you going to join them?" I wave my hand in the general direction our friends have gone.

He snorts. "You think I'm going to rely on them to get us food to last the weekend?" He looks around, surveying the aisles. "Who knows what randomness they will pick out. I'm sticking with the person who knows what they are doing."

Shaking my head, we turn down an aisle containing all sorts of bread. I totally pegged this as a sort of store that would only have white or wheat bread, but the variety is nice.

Out of the corner of my eye I see Derrick staring at me. "What?"

"I bet you have a list of things to buy, don't you?"

Even with all the time that has passed, and how little he knows about me now, he still remembers my little quirks. "Maybe." I wink at him.

One of the wheels on the cart begins to squeak the further we go down the aisle. My gaze wanders over everything as if I don't know what I'm looking for before grabbing a loaf of whole grain bread.

He stares at me, a tiny smirk forming on his lips. As if he knows that I'm acting like I don't know what I'm going to place in the cart. The intensity of his gaze finally breaks my resolve. "Fine, I have a list." I hold up my phone to show him the app I'm using.

He barks out a laugh. "I knew it. Even when we used to hang out, you were always prepared."

"Well," I say. "I like knowing we're going to have food the whole time. I don't want to waste precious camping and lake time by constantly having to go back to the store to pick up something we forgot."

"I wish Cami had given you more notice about the trip. We could have avoided coming to the store altogether."

We gather the rest of the items I have on my list. Cami and Travis are still yet to be seen. I wonder where they went. The store is a lot smaller than the ones we are used to, and we should have bumped into them already. Are they avoiding us?

There isn't much of a line at the checkout and I'm about to ask Derrick to go find the others when they round the corner. Their hands are empty. I assumed they went to get stuff they liked, but there's nothing. I don't miss the small wink Cami shoots Derrick, though. What is that about?

Behind the counter, a girl our age begins scanning our items. She doesn't ask how we're doing or make small talk. That's something new. Anytime we went camping as kids, the people that worked at the stores were also chatty. "Can you add a few bags of ice to that, please?"

She glances up for a brief second, nods, and keys something into the register. I turn to ask everyone if they need to add something when I see Cami pointing her finger toward me and Derrick shaking his head.

"What's going on?"

"Nothing," they reply. Voices too high, and obviously trying to keep me out of the loop.

"Derrick?" The only reason I ask him is because he'll be the first one to break. Cami will go to her grave with things she doesn't want to say. It's a wonder I was able to get her to open up last semester.

Derrick tries to find anything else to look at but me. "She was asking me how the trip was going?"

"She's here. She knows exactly how the trip is going. Why would she be asking you?" My senses are telling me I'm not going to like whatever Derrick has to say.

"Well, um," he scratches the back of his neck and looks down at the floor. "This whole trip is because of you. Well for you." I jerk back and he sees it. "I wanted to take this trip to show you that we are good together, and that we should see what happens between us as more than friends."

My attention snaps to Cami. "Is that true?"

"Yes, I helped him come up with this whole idea. I knew how much you liked camping as a kid, and I figured it would be the perfect thing to get you two to gravitate back to each other."

I stare at her, hoping to find a shred of guilt at tricking me into this whole thing. But, there is none. She feels completely justified in her actions. Derrick on the other hand looks like he's about to pass out. His cheeks are a rosy pink, and there is so much hope in his eyes.

"I can't believe y'all. You've basically tricked me into coming on a mini vacation to get back together."

"For what it's worth, I told them it was a bad idea." Travis chimes in, ever so helpful.

I glare at him. I can't deal with this right now. On one hand it's sweet, but I'm still annoyed. Cami made it sound like it was a last-minute thing and they wanted me to tag along. I wanted a weekend of no stress, and now *this*. I don't give either of them a chance to explain. I turn around and walk right through the front door. The little bell tinkling above it lost in the sounds of my feet hitting the pavement as fast as I can.

derrick

"WHY IN THE hell would you tell her the entire purpose of this trip?" Cami huffs. "We haven't even been here a day, and you have basically destroyed any chance at winning her back."

I stare at the door Darcy stormed out of wondering if I have lost her for good. "I would *love* to stand here and argue with you right now, but I need to go find Darcy." I know she didn't miss my sarcasm because she rolls her eyes at me. One of these days her eyes are going to get stuck like that she does it so much.

Tossing my credit card at Travis, I rush out of the store hoping to catch Darcy before she's gone too far. It's hot out here and she definitely doesn't need to be walking back to the campsite by herself. That whole situation could have gone better. Why did I have to spill everything? Oh yeah, because I word vomit all over the place when she's around. I can't seem to keep my cool when I'm in her presence, and that will most likely be my undoing.

I stop in the small parking lot to search for her, and finally see her in the distance heading straight for the camping grounds. She must've been booking it if she is so far away that she is a speck on the horizon. The amount of guilt I feel right now for tricking her into this trip is insurmountable, and I hope she will forgive me before we leave. I know I should probably give her some space to think things over but I can't in good faith allow her to walk that distance alone.

"Darcy," I yell trying to catch her attention. She doesn't stop or look back. If anything, I think she's walking faster. Never in my life, have I made a girl react that way.

She's obviously not going to make this easy for me, and I don't blame her at all. Droplets of sweat are already forming on my brow as I begin jogging to catch up with her. I have no idea what I'm going to say to her but I hope, at least, she will listen.

"Dammit, Darcy. Will you hold up for just a second?" My voice comes out in a breathless pant as I try to keep the momentum until I'm mere feet away from her.

For a second, I wonder if she heard me, but she stops in her tracks almost causing me to collide with her. "What do you want from me, Derrick?"

"I just want to talk." Cars are flying by us on the main road to get to the lake. There's not even a shoulder for us stand on to keep us away from the traffic. The only thing keeping us from being a casualty is a tiny patch of grass. It's definitely not the safest place for us to have this conversation.

Darcy places her fingertips to her temple as if she's massaging away a headache. "I don't know if I want to talk right now." She crosses her arms over her chest until she notices my eyes are now on the cleavage she is inadvertently showing off. Groaning, she puts her hand on her hip. "You blindsided me in there. I thought this trip was going to be about rebuilding our friendship, hanging out, and having fun. Not some asinine attempt to win me back."

Even though she's bitching at me, and I deserve it, I see a flicker of doubt cross over her face. Like she doesn't completely believe what she's saying. That look right there gives me the courage to lay it all out there.

I widen my legs and cross my arms over my chest, mimicking Darcy's earlier stance. Too bad I don't have any cleavage for her to ogle. But that doesn't stop her from staring at my arms and the way my shirt stretches across my biceps. "Look, I know I was wrong in planning the trip for that specific reason." She opens her mouth but I hold up my hand to silence her. "It's just that, this is the only way I could get you to listen to me and be around me. I want you to take a chance to really see me, and not that boy who unknowingly hurt you. And don't say you don't have feelings for me anymore because that's bullshit."

"Excuse me, you don't know, or get to tell me, how I

feel." Her face is bright red and I know I have completely pissed her off, but I'm not backing down.

"Actually, I do. You think I don't see the way you look at me. Like you miss me and hate me all at the same time. The way your eyes tell a different story than your words? Let's not forget that I see you. I *see* you, Darcy. You may have gotten rid of all of your old clothes, and everything else, but you're still the same girl I fell for last summer." The superhero shirt she's wearing is a small hint of the "old" Darcy trying to reappear. Taking a deep breath, I level her with a stare. "I told you that day in your room that I would be there for you in any form you'll have me. I'm not going to lie, I want to be more than friends. But, if that's what you really want, then I'll stop. I'll push thoughts of you to the back of my mind and move on."

I exhale and feel a huge weight lifted off my shoulders. She's completely silent, eyes glued to me, and I'm not sure I've even gotten through to her. But I tried. My feelings are out in the open, and it's up to her to decide what she is going to do with them.

A car pulls up beside us and I don't bother seeing who is inside. Instead, I study Darcy, trying to puzzle out what she is thinking. It's not until I hear my name that I turn around.

"Do y'all want to get in the car? It's hot as hell out here and we're heading back to the campsite." Travis calls out from his partially open window. He looks like a total creeper, peering over the tinted glass, in his attempt to keep the cool air inside the car.

I look to Darcy to see what she is going to do. When she stays silent I turn to walk around the back to get in the backseat on the side that is facing traffic. My hand is on the handle when I hear her call out, "Wait."

Standing on my tiptoes I look over the SUV. Darcy is giving me a look that says "what the hell are you doing, we aren't finished here." I let go of the handle and head toward the front of the car, passing a very confused Cami in the front passenger seat.

Now that Darcy has my attention, she looks at Travis. "I think we're going to walk." I don't even question her. I just jog the rest of the way until I am by her side. All the while, a flame of hope burns through my insides.

"You're going to what?" Cami asks incredulously. "You're going to end up passing out from heat stroke, or something, if you walk all the way back. I mean, we may be approaching Fall, but that means jack shit in Texas."

"I'm willing to take my chances," Darcy says defiantly. "Besides, he and I have a few things we need to discuss." She begins walking toward the back of the SUV but stops. Turning back, she stares pointedly at Cami. "And, you and I need to have a talk, too." She doesn't say anything else, but continues to the back of the car, opens the hatch and grabs a couple of bottles of water. She tosses one at me and stops, again, at Travis's still open window. "We will be fine. If we aren't there in thirty minutes, you have my permission to send out a search party."

I can see through the opening that Cami isn't on board with this plan. However, she sighs. "Fine, but if you are not back at the campsite in exactly thirty minutes, I'm coming to look for you."

Darcy simply nods and backs away from the car. I see Travis wave before quickly rolling up his window and driving off. Darcy is way too calm and collected, and I don't know if I trust that. I know this girl's love of zombie shows and all the "useful," but slightly terrifying things she learns from them. I'll be lucky if I make it back to the campsite with her. For all I know she has some sort of devious plan up her sleeve.

"Start walking," she playful shoves my shoulder. "Cami's serious. She *will* send people to look for me if we aren't back in time."

"Are you kidding me?" I know, even though Cami has been trying to help me with the whole Darcy situation, she's insanely protective of her. I just didn't realize it was quite that intense.

"Nope," she replies. "She had a few scares back when she used to party all the time, and now she's super anal about knowing what's going on and who I'm with. It's almost like having a second mom." She shrugs, "It can be annoying but at least I know she cares."

"That's good. I'm glad you have someone that has your back." The heat is relentless, and I take a swig of my water, grateful that Darcy thought to get some before she sent our friends on their way.

"Speaking of," she drawls. "We need to talk."

I'm terrified of what she's going to say. That she'll insist on this whole friendship thing, and I really will have to figure out how to move on from her. I don't want that...at all. But I'm not going to pressure her if that's her request. I don't reply. I survey our surroundings, hoping like hell that we're getting close to our destination. We pass a sign that says two miles, and I'm beginning to wish we'd taken Travis up on his offer.

"Why didn't you tell me all of that the first time we talked?"

I snort. I can't help it, she's seriously asking this question? "Um, because anytime I try to talk to you about anything that doesn't pertain to school, you run."

"I do not."

I begin ticking off fingers. "I tell you what happened that summer in the gym, you ran. I bring your yoga mat back to you and we were so awkward that I didn't want to kill what little hope I had of winning you back. You cut your break short at work because you couldn't sit with me for fifteen minutes. You *are* a runner."

"That's because I don't know how to be with you without being that reserved nerdy girl I was before college."

"What's so wrong with being nerdy?"

"I thought that was why you stood me up. You didn't want to be seen with the awkward geek anymore. That's why I reinvented myself. I didn't want to give anyone else the ability to hurt me again."

"Well," I grab her hand, shocked when she doesn't yank it away. "I happen to like the Darcy that told me the plot of whatever comic she was reading. Don't let me or anyone else change who you really are. You need to be comfortable and happy with yourself."

"Oh, no buddy." She begins to pull her hand out of mine, but I squeeze it gently and she stops. "You don't get to change the subject."

"I'm not, you're the one who brought it up."

"And, I'm the one getting us back on topic." I don't miss that she walks a little bit closer to me, even with the heat pressing down on us. "I'm still pissed, *but* I can understand why you thought you needed this elaborate plan." She waves her free hand in the air, meaning this whole situation. "I probably would have come around eventually. You know that, right?"

"I didn't want to take that chance." I stop walking, pulling her close to me. "I meant everything I said back there. I didn't date anyone the year I stayed home. All I was focused on, besides letting Mom take care of me because she likes to, is how I was going to make the basketball team and wondering if I was ever going to see you again. I was shocked when I found out you were Cami's best friend. And that date didn't go at all like I had hoped."

"Yeah, I wasn't quite over my heartbreak." She looks up, eyes on mine, and I can see how much she regrets behaving like a crazy person. "Why didn't you come to Hilltown last year?"

"Do you remember that tryout I was supposed to go to for the team?" She nods. "Well, that was on the same day as Gramps's funeral so I didn't make it. Mom took it as a sign that I needed to be home for the year, until I got my bearings."

Darcy laughs. "Sorry, the tryouts isn't funny. Just your mom's reactions. You *are* her baby boy, so I can sort of see where she's coming from." She leans into me. Sweat dampens both of our shirts, but neither of us cares. "You'll make the team. You're awesome, and I know you'll do great."

"So," I don't want to bring it up now, but I need to know. "Where does that leave us?"

"I'm not sure. Between work, classes, and the fact that I know you'll make the team, I'm not sure when we would even have time for each other."

I place my hand on her cheek. "We make time for each other. That's what people who want to be in a relationship do." Her eyes are wide, and I can see the fear and doubt swirl within them. "How about we date and take it day by day. If it gets to be too much for you, I'll back off and do my best to be a friend."

Darcy squints her eyes, mulling the idea over. She doesn't answer for a long time, and finally she says, "Okay. I think I can work with that."

Pulling her into my arms, I breathe a sigh of relief. And, I also hope I don't smell as bad as I fear from sweating. I'm about to pull her closer for a kiss when her phones dings.

"That's most likely Cami. We better get back before she makes good on her threat." She squeezes my hand, and I can't stop the broad smile taking over my face. We can do this. At least, I hope we can because I don't think I can let her go again.

darcy

CAMI IS ALREADY at the camp entrance when we finally made it back. "Where the hell have you been? We left over an hour ago, you told me thirty minutes. You're lucky I didn't do anything drastic like call the police." She's marching toward us, face bright red, and fury spilling from her mouth.

"We are here, there's no need to freak out." I do my best to make my voice as soft and gentle as possible. Talking to her as if she is a small bright child in order to calm her nerves. I can tell it's working because she visibly relaxes and is no longer stomping toward us.

But then Derrick opens his mouth. "Yeah, Mom."

I've never seen someone turn so freaking fast. Her head snaps to Derrick and the glare she shoots him is enough to scare the hell out of anyone. Derrick steps back, putting his hands up in surrender.

He definitely doesn't want the wrath of Cami. She

can be awesome or terrifying. I prefer that she be in a good mood. "Um, why don't you go ahead and catch up with Travis? Cam and I will be there in a few."

He glances at Cami, who is giving him the stink eye. "That's a good idea." He bends down, brushing a kiss across my cheek before jogging off.

Cami's eyebrow quirks up. "I'm guessing the walk went well." I hook my arm through hers and spin her in the opposite direction of our campsite. "Where are we going?"

"To talk." I reply. "I told you we were going to have a discussion."

"I was kind of hoping you'd be all lovey dovey and kind of forget about it." She sighs, "apparently there's no luck in that happening."

"Nope. I didn't let him off the hook, and I'm not letting you either."

"Okay, I guess I deserve it." She's looking anywhere but at me. I abruptly stop, causing her to trip over her feet, and almost faceplant. I can't stop the giggle from bubbling up. I'm usually the clumsy one, it nice when she's caught off guard. "That's not funny, asshole."

"It was a little funny." I snort. "And it takes an asshole to know one."

"I thought we were out here for you to bitch me out."

"You know I'm not going to bitch you out...much." The campgrounds are full of life. Not just those of the people sitting in groups chatting, but also the sounds of summer. Birds chirping, bugs zipping about. The serenity I've always felt about being outside hits me, and I'm not even mad at Cami and Derrick for dragging me out here under false pretenses. I needed this.

"Hello, Darcy," Cami snaps her fingers in front of my face. "I'm ready for my lecture."

"Smartass," I mumble.

She bumps into me. "I heard that."

"I meant for you to." I inhale and exhale, taking my sweet time, not sure how to voice both my frustration and elation about being here. "Look, I was pretty upset earlier when I stormed out of the grocery store. When I found out that you were behind this whole thing, I was hurt. You're supposed to look out for me, and I felt like you chose him over me."

"I didn't mean to make you feel that way," Cami whispers. "I just wanted you to be happy. I know you still have feelings for him. I can tell by the way you clam up when you're around each other. You get all nervous and shy. And, you are all that Derrick talks about. If I had any doubts about how he feels about you, I never would have agreed to this."

I wrap my arms around her, pulling her into a sweaty hug. "I understand that now, just maybe next time let me and him figure it out on our own. Even if he brings you into his shenanigans. I would have eventually found my way back to him." I release her and take a step back. "Thank you, though. For talking me into coming out here. I needed this. The open air and a small taste of my childhood are actually doing me some good."

"That's good." She squeezes my hand. "I'm happy some good has come of it. So... what happened on your walk that had Derrick giving you a kiss on the cheek?"

"We talked." I shrug. "More like he laid his heart on the line and left the decision up to me."

"I'm assuming you said yes to being with him."

"Yep. At some point I would have had to stop fighting it. What better time than now? Especially after his declaration of love. I felt like Julia Stiles when Heath Ledger hires the marching band to show her how he feels in *10 Things I Hate About You*."

Cami puts the back of her hand to her forehead. "Catch me, I may faint from all the swoony sentiments."

"Shut up," I swat at her. "I just hope this is the right decision. That I won't regret it later on."

"You've got this girl." She slings her arm over my shoulder, turning me back in the direction we need to be walking. "Besides, if he breaks your heart, I'll make his life a living hell."

"Why do I feel like that isn't an empty threat?"

"Because it's not." She leans into me. "I would do anything for my girls when they are hurting. Even if that means throat punching the assholes that hurt them."

"I'm so happy we were assigned as roommates."

"Me too," Cami smiles. "You're so lucky to have a friend like me."

I unscrew the lid on the bottle of water I'm still holding, pretending like I'm going to take a drink. "The luckiest." I pour the water on her head and take off running. "I'll see you at the site."

"Dammit, Darcy." She's laughing so I know she isn't too upset. "You better not have gotten my phone wet."

I hear her feet pounding the dirt behind me, close to catching up with me. I am the lucky one. I never had very many friends in high school. She's the first real friend I've ever had, and she'll accept me for me.

My side is burning from running without stretching. This is what college is supposed to be about, making memories with friends and having fun. Maybe Tom was right in calling me uptight. I feel all the stress I've put on myself fall from my shoulders. I'm going to do my best to get back to the girl I used to be. The one that looked at the world with optimism and didn't hide all her weird and quirkiness. It's time for this girl to embrace her weird once again.

It has been forever since I have stayed up this late or been this exhausted. But, it feels good. Today has been full of memories that I know I will keep and cherish forever. These moments definitely make the trip worthwhile, even if it was a ruse to get me to talk to Derrick.

All of my things are now in the tent I am sharing with Derrick. He hasn't made it back from the bathroom, or wherever it was he went, yet. I roll out my sleeping bag and recount the events of the day to help squash my nerves.

When Cami and I finally made it back to the campsite our neighbors, the Campbells, were talking to the guys. I could tell from the way Derrick's eyes lit up in excitement that we would be doing something fun and adventurous. We spent the entire day on Mr. and Mrs. Campbell's pontoon boat fishing, talking, and just enjoying each other's company. I didn't even know they had a boat, but apparently it was sitting at the dock waiting to be taken out on the lake. The highlight of my day was watching Cami attempt to bait her own hook. There are moments when I see Cami and all I see is a strong badass woman, this wasn't one of those moments. I think she may have even gagged a little bit. It shouldn't be funny, but it is. Only because she likes to be as self-sufficient as possible, and this is the one time I've seen her ask for help lately. Mrs. Campbell kept asking her if she was alright, or if she needed her to do it. But Cami would only ask for Travis's help, too embarrassed to be shown up by an older lady.

Derrick pops his head into the tent. "Are you okay in here?"

It's then that I realize I'm standing still, the corners of my sleeping bag in my hands, and I'm grinning goofily into space. "Yeah, just picturing Cami's face when we were fishing earlier."

He chuckles, "I don't think she is ever going to want to go fishing again."

"She might," I say. "I think she liked the fishing part. She even caught quite a few. She just wasn't a fan of the whole preparation thing."

He pulls the sleeping bag out of my hand. "Here, let me help you with that."

"It's okay, I can do it."

"I know you can do it, I just want to help. Which side do you want?" Derrick gestures to the half open partition.

Instead of answering, I unzip it the rest of the way, tying the extra fabric to the side, until there is no longer a barrier. A part of me wants to rush and put the partition back in place, if only to let me hide from my emotions for a few more hours. But, I did promise Derrick I would try, and take things as they come.

"Are you sure?" He finishes laying out the sleeping bag. "I don't want you to feel pressured, or think you have to sleep next to me. I'm totally okay with us having separate spaces."

"I'm sure." I nod, hoping it makes my whispered statement more believable. And, I am sure. The memory of being snuggled up in his arms last year surfaces. It was comfortable, and more importantly, I felt safe.

"Do you need anything else before I close the front flap?"

"Nope, I'm good. Just really tired." My mouth opens in a wide yawn, driving the point home. I sit down on top of my sleeping bag, eyeing the gap he's left between our bedding. "Why don't we unzip one of them all the way, and use the other to cover up?"

"W-we can do that," he stutters. "I just didn't want to make any assumptions. I'm willing to go at whatever pace you're comfortable with."

A giggle spills from my lips. "It's not like we're going to have sex or anything. I'm perfectly capable of sleeping with you without, you know, *sleeping* with you. As long as you can control yourself."

His face is beet red. It's not often that I leave people speechless, but I revel in this small victory. "That's not what I meant." The words rush out of his mouth, as if the faster he says them the faster it will hide his embarrassment.

"I know that, genius." I push my sleeping bag to the side and began unzipping his. Spreading it out until it almost takes up the entire floor space of the tent. Mine is much smaller so it doesn't take long before it's flat. I pat the space beside me, inviting him to lie down with me.

I wince when he hesitates realizing that the action could be suggestive. Hell, it could even be seen as pathetic. But my insecurities are shoved aside when he takes his shirt off and joins me on the blanket.

Derrick lies down on his side, leaving space between us, allowing me to decide how close I want to be to him. There's one thing that I can always say about him. He knows how to behave like a gentleman. He's never been one to push my boundaries.

I close the gap between us, my back pressed against

his chest. He wraps his arm around my stomach, gently caressing the sliver of skin where my shirt has ridden up. I've missed this, being tangled in his arms, knowing that he'll respect my boundaries and make me feel like I'm the most special person in his world.

Shifting to get closer to him, I flinch in pain. "Are you okay?" His voice is laced with concern, determined to do whatever I need him to do so that I feel better.

"Yeah," I whisper into the darkness. "I must have gotten too much sun today. My back is on fire."

"Hold on." I feel the loss when he moves away. Moments later he's back, and I hear a lid flip open.

Before I have a chance to ask what he's doing, a cold wet glob hits my back. "Shit, that's cold."

"Sorry," he begins rubbing the aloe into my skin, slowly soothing the pain away. "I'm glad I thought to pick some aloe up before we came out here."

"Me too. Thank you"

He pulls me close to him, and I'm thankful my sunburn doesn't hurt right this second. "Go to sleep," he whispers in my ear. "There's no telling what the Campbell's have in store for us tomorrow."

I close my eyes. Sleep finding me faster than the night before. I could definitely get used to this.

derrick

DARCY SHIFTS in my arms pulling me from my sleep. Having her beside me all night was pure heaven, and I hope it becomes a regular occurrence. It's definitely something I could get used to.

I roll to my back trying to find a more comfortable position without waking Darcy. To my surprise the sleeping bag is wet, and I can feel it begin to soak into my shirt. Why is it wet in here? We didn't bring any drinks to bed with us, so I know it can't be because something spilled. My sleep addled mind finally makes sense of the soft pitter-pattering coming from outside the tent. It's raining, of course it is. Mr. weather guy, nor the app, said anything about rain this weekend when we checked. But from the dampness spreading over our sleeping bag, and the wet floor of the tent, it appears it's been raining almost all night.

"Darcy," I shake her shoulders, trying to rouse her

from her sleep. "Wake up. We have a slight problem." Slight might be an understatement depending on how she reacts. She could be completely fine with it, or she could lose her shit. I'm betting on the former.

She stirs, bringing her hands to her eyes and rubbing the sleep out of them. She stretches her arms over her head which has her back planted more firmly into the ground. Her eyes widened, shocked and maybe a bit freaked out. "What in the hell is that?"

I smirk, not even minding the fact I'm still getting wet because of the rain. "Listen." I point my finger at ceiling of our tent, indicating where the sound is coming from.

When she hears the sound of steady droplets hitting the roof of the tent she groans. "Ugh, why didn't we know about this? Did you know it was supposed to rain?"

"Well, when we checked the weather last week there was zero chance of rain. I didn't think to check it after that. I mean, we live in Texas... we're almost always in a drought. Maybe next time we should look at it a couple of days before we go camping."

"I like how you assume there's going to be a next time." Darcy is rummaging through her bag for who knows what. "Cami is going to freak out if she isn't already. This is totally going to turn her off from camping in the future."

"Who said anything about Travis and Cami coming along next time?"

Finally finding what she is looking for she pulls out a

small plastic square. Unfolding it she replies, "who said I wanted to go on another camping trip with you?" She's pulling the plastic over her head so I can't see her face to tell whether she is joking or not. But when her head comes through the now visible hole, she's smiling. I sigh in relief, glad she wasn't being serious.

I watch her pull the hood of the plastic poncho over her hair and can't help grinning. This girl is always prepared and I should have known that a little rain wouldn't bring her down. "You'll be lucky if I invite you to my next camping trip. I'm sure I can find someone willing to come with me." I continue teasing.

She points at my shorts, becoming wetter the longer we sit here, and says, "I'm not entirely sure you would survive without me. Cami was right when she said y'all *needed* me on this trip. Y'all didn't even have a real plan for *food*."

I open my mouth to list all the reasons why I would in fact survive when a shriek pierces through the air.

"And," Darcy drawls. "Cami is awake." She quickly grabs another poncho from her duffel bag and begins unzipping the tent flap. "I'll be right back." Before I can say anything else she rushes out of the tent to calm her friend down. She deserves a "best friend of the year" award. Cami is awesome, but sometimes she freaks out about the smallest things. I'm always shocked when they tell me she didn't used to be this way. I respect her for standing on her own two feet and getting out from under her dad. She just needs to take a breather every once in a while.

I'm actually surprised it took this long for the rain and wet floors to wake Cami up. Every time she has stayed at our dorm she's been a light sleeper so I figured she would have woken up much sooner. At least before us. But it took us a while to wake up, and I can't throw stones when we didn't know it was raining. Glancing at Darcy's duffel bag I spy two more small plastic squares, and I'm relieved that she thought to get rain ponchos for all of us. I scoop them up, pause long enough to close the tent, even though it won't help much, and jog to Travis and Cami's tent.

"I don't care what the forecast says, I think we should cut our losses and head home early." Cami is on one of her tangents and it'll be next to impossible to change her mind about leaving. The plus side to that is I'll get a little bit more practice in for basketball tryouts. Or, Darcy and I could go to Austin and have a date day. I'm pretty sure I can figure out something that doesn't involve being outdoors. If I'm lucky, the rain will stop and I can find something for us to do outside.

Darcy is doing her best to soothe Cami, but even she knows arguing is a lost cause. "That's fine with me. I'm sure I have some homework that I missed that needs to be done." She sits on her knees, and points to the clothes strewn about the tent. "Let's get everything packed up and then we can get on the road."

Cami doesn't argue or complain, she begins shoving her things into a bag and sloppily rolling up the sleeping bag. I can see Darcy cringe at the mess Cami has made of the bedding and I know she is just itching to fix it.

"Why don't you and Travis go make room in the car?" I point outside where it is still raining. Darcy and I can get everything packed that much faster without the grumpy people underfoot. She doesn't respond but reaches for Travis's hand and they duck out of the tent together. That was easier than I thought. I assumed she would gripe about having to get stuff done in the rain. I guess she wants to get out of here as fast as possible. Between the bug, baiting her own hook, and now the rain, she's done with this whole trip.

As soon as they're out of the tent Darcy begins unrolling the sleeping bags, straightening them up only to re-roll them. They look almost as if they just came from the store, tightly bundled and so freaking small. There's no way I would have been able to do that. My sleeping bag would look like a fluffy square from folding it.

When our bags and bedding are shoved into the back of Travis's SUV, Darcy makes quick work of disassembling the tent. I'm in awe at how quickly she does it. It would've taken me at least an hour to get the tent put away. Before long we are back on the road heading home. Hopefully we don't make a pit stop at the creepy gas station along the way. Or if we have to stop, it will be a well-lit gas station with a ton of other people there.

The steady rain hits the top of the car, relaxing me. Darcy is sitting on the opposite side of the seat from me, and I pull her closer. She startles but rests her head on my shoulder and within minutes she's fast asleep. I'm already racking my brain for things Darcy and I can do tomorrow. There is no way I'm letting her hide away in her room to do homework.

I have never been so happy to see my tiny dorm room bed, as I am right now. We dropped the girls off and carried their things upstairs before heading home. My body is sore from sleeping on the hard ground. The sleeping bags barely adding a barrier between me and the rough terrain. The next camping trip I go on, I am investing in an air mattress. If I've learned one thing on our whole two-day trip, it's that comfort is key.

I've barely thrown my laundry into the dirty clothes hamper when there's a knock at our door. I glanced at Travis, "Are you expecting anybody?"

He shakes his head and flops face first onto his bed. I guess that means I'm getting the door. A part of me hopes it is Darcy and that she couldn't wait to see me again. I open the door with a wide smile that quickly drops when I see who is standing there. It's definitely not who I was expecting.

"Where the hell have you been all weekend?" Bentley demands.

"I went camping with my friends. Why?" I'm not going to lie, I'm a little pissed off that he's here and being a total douchebag right now.

"Because," he pokes my chest. "I thought you were serious about wanting to make the basketball team. If you were, you wouldn't have been gallivanting in the woods. Instead, you would have been on the court working on your shot."

"I am serious." Who does this guy think he is? I was grateful when he agreed to train me, but that doesn't mean I can't have a life off the court. "There are still two months before basketball season starts, and I didn't think taking off three days would be a huge deal. I'm already coming in early before classes to practice, and I'm on the court every day after my last class working on improving my game.

"Look, I'm sorry for being so hard on you. But this isn't high school anymore, you're going to have to bring better than your "A" game to make the team and actually get playing time." I know I should listen to him. He's a senior and knows what he's talking about, but that doesn't stop what he's saying from ruffling my feathers.

"You think I don't know that?" I lean on the doorjamb trying to get comfortable, but also trying to keep the frustration out of my stance. "I'm doing the best that I can, but I need some sort of downtime, too, or else I'm going to burnout and give up on the whole thing altogether."

Bentley holds his hands up as a weird sort of peace offering. "I completely understand, and I can respect that. But I better see you in the practice gym first thing Tuesday morning."

He doesn't wait for a response or seem to care what I might say. He knows I'll be there because he knows how much I want this. It's barely after three so I can get in a couple of hours on the court tonight so that I'm not quite so rusty Tuesday morning. I set an alarm on my phone, and close my eyes finally feeling comfortable enough to get some actual sleep. I need a power nap before I hit the court and decide what I'm going to do with Darcy tomorrow.

darcy

TAP. *Tap. Tap.* What in the world is that noise? Is someone knocking? The sound is light, barely enough to pull me out of my sleep. But now my eyes are wide open. The clock on my nightstand says it's nine in the morning. I haven't slept this late in ages, and whoever is on the other side of that door better have a damn good reason for waking me up. It's not often that I get this luxury.

"Cami, are you going to get that?" When she doesn't answer I glance toward her side of the room. Her bed is empty, and her comforter lies in a jumbled heap at the foot of her bed. That's weird, she is so not a morning person and whatever got her out of bed had to of been something worth her time. The only time she's up before noon is when we have to open at the coffee shop. I guess I'll have to get the door.

The knocking stops for a few seconds and I lie still hoping the unexpected visitor will go away. When the annoying sound of knuckles on wood starts again, I groan. I'm not normally a moody morning person, but after the craziness of this weekend I could use a few more hours of sleep. Even though I had fun while we were at the lake, the emotional lows and highs took their toll on me.

Pushing my blankets aside I take a quick inventory of what I'm wearing. Sleep shorts and a tank top, everything is covered so this will have to be presentable enough for whoever's outside of my door.

I swing open the door, perhaps a bit harder than necessary, and gasp when I see who is standing on the other side. "Wh-what are you doing here?"

Derrick leans against the door jamb and shoves his hands in his pocket. He should not look this good this early in the morning. His hair is still damp and styled in a way that looks like he just rolled out of bed. "Well, I tried calling but you didn't answer."

"My phone never rang." I rush over to my nightstand where I put my phone before I went to sleep. I tap the button to see my notifications and suck in a breath when I see that Derrick has, in fact, called me. Five times to be exact. I tilt the phone to the side and see that it is on silent. When did I put it on silent? I never do that in case there's an emergency at home and someone needs to get ahold of me. And then it hits me, I didn't want to be bothered this morning so I put the phone on silent to ensure that it didn't happen.

"I hope it's okay that I just showed up," Derrick says

from much closer than the door. Crap, I forgot I left the door wide open. I whip around to face Derrick and catch his eyes roving over my body and all the skin I have on display. Double crap. I don't blame him for it and I *am* the one putting my body out there on display. But, had I known he was going to come over I would've worn something a little more modest. Something along the lines of what I wore when we went camping, capri yoga pants and a T-shirt. They were comfortable, cool, and didn't make me seem like I was crying out for his attention. I feel naked, right now. Like he can see through the thin clothing to what's underneath.

I rush to my closet door where my robe is hanging on a hook, yank it off, and slip it on. "Oh, um, yeah that's fine." I hope I don't sound as flustered as I really am. The warmth spreading through my cheeks is a clear indicator that I am most likely blushing. He has to know how he affects me. "Sorry I missed your phone call. What's up?" I'm going for casual, but the words come out breathy and shaken.

"What are you doing today?"

"I *was* sleeping, until someone rudely woke me up. Then I was going to try to get ahead in some of my classes." I sit on the edge of my bed and pull my blanket over me. Not only trying to hide my legs, but also to ease my nerves. I've had this blanket since I was a toddler, and it is literally a security blanket that I still use to this day.

"Yeah, you aren't going to spend the day doing homework." He says pinning me with a stare that brooks no argument. Too bad, I don't back down quite so easily to commands.

"And, what exactly will I be doing?" I cross my arms over my chest, not caring if the motion accentuates the little bit of cleavage I actually have.

"You're going out with me. On a date." Grabbing the shower caddy from where it sits on the floor beside my closet, he hands it to me and points to the door, which is still freaking open. "Go get ready."

"Just because we're dating doesn't mean you get to boss me around." I huff. "That's not how relationships work." But, I stand and grab the caddy anyway. "I don't remember you being this bossy when we dated before."

"That's because you weren't playing hard to get then. Now I actually have to work to keep your attention." He takes the spot I just vacated on my bed. "Get a move on. We're burning daylight."

"First off, what am I supposed to wear? I have no clue where we are even going." I pause hoping he'll answer. "Second, can't you wait for me in your own dorm room? You make me nervous just sitting in my room."

"Nope, I'm good. If I go back to my room, there's a good chance you'll bail on me." I scoff at that. I wouldn't do that, but I haven't given him any reassurance to the contrary. "As for what to wear, comfortable and casual is the way to go. We aren't doing anything fancy."

"Fine," I mumble. I grab the door knob on my way out to shut it behind me, but I pause and stick my head back into my room. "You are going to have to leave my room while I get dressed. As much as I like you, I'm not ready for you to see all the goods."

He's laughing as I shut the door. "It's not like you were hiding them too well with what you're wearing." He says it just loud enough for me to hear him through the door.

I stomp toward the community bathroom on our floor. He is insufferable. I'm trying to figure out what drew me to him in the first place. It wasn't only his good looks...though that didn't hurt. It was his sense of humor and how comfortable he is being himself. I used to be that way, and I lost myself when I lost him. I know exactly what I'm going to wear for our date. It'll be a reminder to the both of us of what we once were.

I'm pleasantly surprised when I get back to the room and Derrick isn't there. This may be the one time he hasn't made good on his promise. It's not that I don't want him here, it's just he makes me nervous, and there's no way I would be able to get ready without feeling self-conscious. And now, I don't know if I should be happy or upset that he isn't sitting on my bed where I left him. In his place, though, I find a piece of paper with pink scribbles across it.

Meet me in the commons area when you are done getting ready. Remember casual and comfortable.

~Derrick.
PS: if you aren't down here in one hour, I'll be back at your door.
PPS: What is with all the colorful pens? I couldn't find a normal one anywhere.

Really? His main focus is the color of my pen collection? I shake my head. This boy continues to surprise me every single day. As weird and immature as it probably sounds, I don't want to throw this note in the trash. If things go south with us I'll need something to remember him by. Even though I'm usually pretty optimistic, I can't fight the doubt in the back of my head that it's only a matter of time before this whole thing blows up in our faces. I grab the note and slide it in the back of one of my journals. It can stay there until I figure out another space for it.

The closet door is still open from when Cami was in there this morning. I swear that girl never closes anything. Standing in the doorway, I peer at the clothes hanging side-by-side in pristine order. I usually complain about how messy Cami's side of the closet is but looking at my side only shows boring repetition. There's nothing exciting about my clothes. None of this is going to work for my date with Derrick. Luckily, the box of long forgotten clothes is still sitting on the floor of the closet. I rummage through it until I find the perfect shirt. Paired with some shorts and my Vans, it'll be the perfect ensemble for the girl I used to be.

Getting dressed doesn't take long, but I have no clue what to do with my hair. Even though it stopped raining last night I'm sure it is still humid outside. As much as I would love to fix my hair, it would be a lost cause. Rather than throwing my hair into a messy bun, I begin separating the strands for a side braid. I'm nervous about being alone with Derrick since it's the first time we will be out together after deciding to date, and I'll need a hairstyle that will bring out my confidence. The side braid is similar to that of the mother of dragons from *Game of Thrones*, and I need all the strength and encouragement I can get from mimicking her badassery. I put on a little bit of mascara and lip-gloss, deciding that is as glammed up as I'm going to get today. He said casual, and I'm taking that to heart.

Derrick is nowhere to be seen in the commons area. He said an hour, and I know I'm a few minutes early, but I assumed he would be here waiting for me. What if he ditched me? I'm not sure I can go through that embarrassment and heartache all over again.

My phone in hand, I pull up his name so I can text him. Hopefully he still has the same phone number because I didn't think to double check with him. Maybe I should do that, if this ends up being a wrong number. I begin typing "where are," but I see him walk through the door. He has a bundle of flowers in one hand and the other is shoved in his pocket.

I approach him cautiously, attempting to hide my

excitement about the flowers. "I thought you said it wasn't a fancy date."

He pulls his hand out of his pocket and slinks his arm over my shoulders "Who said they were for you?"

"Oh, so you just go around passing out flowers to strangers?"

"No," he chuckles. "I only give them to the most beautiful girls I know."

I roll my eyes. "That may be the cheesiest line I've ever heard."

Before I can say anything else he bends down and places a chaste kiss on my lips. He holds the flowers in front of me. "These, are for you. The most beautiful girl I know."

Swoon. Even when he's being cocky and overbearing he still knows how to be incredibly sweet.

"Thank you," I whisper. We're about to head out the front door when I realize that I don't want to have to carry these flowers around all day. "Hold on, I should probably go put these in some water in my room."

Derrick blushes and scratches the back of his neck. "I didn't think about that when I bought them for you. But, it's probably a good idea."

"I'll be right back. I promise, I won't take too long." I practically skip on my way to the elevator feeling like a lovesick child. Just as I get to the elevator, the doors open and I'm thankful that I don't have to wait. A girl rushes by me, obviously in a hurry, and I step to the side to get out of her way. Once I'm inside, and the doors are securely closed, I put the flowers to my face and take a deep breath, basking in the sweet smell of the wild-flowers.

I don't have any vases, so I grab the biggest cup we have in our cabinet and fill it with water. Placing the makeshift vase on my desk, I smell them one more time, before locking the room up again.

I run down the stairs, not wanting to wait on the elevators. I almost collide with Derrick when I exit the stairwell. He catches me in his arms, bringing me to his chest. "Are you ready to go?" He whispers into my hair.

"Yep. Let's see what you have in store for me."

He grabs my hand, leading me toward the door. "You wore my favorite shirt."

It's the one he bought me the first time we dated. Loki is standing with his arms crossed and one eyebrow quirked. We always have disagreements on who we think is better *Marvel* or *Justice League*. But I like Loki. Mostly because he's hot, but also because he's a complex villain.

I nod, not knowing what to say, and we exit the building. I was right, the air is muggy and not at all hair friendly. I don't know what we're doing today, but I'm going to push my plans aside, and live in the moment.

derrick

THE DRIVE to Austin goes by quickly. I expected a ton of traffic with people heading home from their Labor Day festivities. I'm not complaining, though. It means more time to sweep Darcy off her feet.

"How is basketball training going?" Her voice startles me. She's been quiet the entire time, watching cars and buildings as we pass by them. She hasn't once asked me where we are going or what we're doing. I thought I would be peppered with questions on the ride, but she's been sitting in her seat, content with the easy silence. Should I be worried? New Darcy has to know exactly what she's doing. Maybe she's letting loose and allowing pieces of her former self to seep through.

"It's going okay. Bentley, the guy that's helping me, showed up at my dorm yesterday pissed because I took the weekend off." I turn the blinker on, getting in the lane we need to be in.

"Are you not allowed to have time off?"

"Yeah," I shrug. "But, he wants me practicing as much as I can. Since I'm coming in a year later, I have to *really* impress the coaches." I've never had any sort of performance anxiety, but I can feel the panic of not making the team bubble up. Tryouts are two months away and it's starting to feel real.

"You'll do great." Her smile is wide when I glance at her. "This is your passion, something you've wanted for a long time. I have faith in you."

I take the ramp for the exit we need and feel some of the worry die down. "I'm glad you do, because I'm freaking out."

Darcy grabs my hand, giving it a gentle squeeze. The reassurance means everything, and I'm happy I have her on my side again. "Are we almost there?"

"Yeah, we're close." She's practically bouncing with excitement about our date. I guess the nerves and annoyance from earlier wore off. "You're not curious what we're doing today?"

"I am." Her fingers are tapping an unsteady rhythm on her leg. Yep, at least some of the nerves are still there. "I'm trying to live in the moment, and not have everything planned out so rigidly."

"That's good. Kind of reminds me of the old times." Winking at her I pull into a parking spot. Her eyes grow wide at the location. Is that a good, or bad, reaction? Did I just royally fuck up? "What do you think?"

"I've never been to a place like this before. I mean, my

dad has gone a few times, but I thought it was for boring dad types to get away from their families." She stills, and glances at me from the corner of her eye. "That's not what this is, is it?"

I laugh. I can't help it. I almost tell her that it's exactly what it is, but I don't. She may very well punch me if I do. "No, that's not what this place is. They have mini golf courses, cornhole, and a golf driving range. We can do whatever you want."

She unbuckles her seatbelt and is out of the car before I even turn the engine off. When I open my door, she's already there waiting for me. She throws her arms around my neck, pulling me down for a kiss. "I want to do it all."

This girl is like a kid on Christmas morning. I'm ecstatic that I've surprised her in a good way for once.

"Am I doing this right?" Darcy is standing in one of the driving stalls, club in hand and shoulders hunched. The tip of her tongue poking out between her lips as she concentrates on the golf ball sitting atop the tiny plastic tea.

I come up behind her so that I can fix her stance because her feet are way too close together. Placing my hands on her hips, I hear a sharp intake of breath. Her entire body tenses for a few seconds before relaxing into my grip. This girl is going to be the death of me and she doesn't even know it. I can't help the way my body reacts to her, or the way my heart beats frantically anytime I'm around her.

"You need to widen your legs some. Your feet are too close together," I whisper in her ear. Her body shivers in response, hopefully in a good way. When she leans into me, I know we aren't going to get through this golf lesson. Not that I'm qualified to teach her shit about golf, I've only played twice in my entire life. Fake it 'til you make it, right?

She shifts her feet placing them further apart. "Like this?"

The way her body brushes against mine leaves me speechless for a few seconds. I've always had the ability to come up with something witty, but all thoughts leave my brain. All I can focus on is the way she feels in my arms and how close she is to me. Then I mentally curse because we are surrounded by people, and I can't be having these thoughts in public or things will become embarrassing.

"Derrick?" Darcy turns her head to look up at me, eyes bright and expression hopeful. "Is this how I'm supposed to stand?"

Shaking the lustful thoughts of my head, I smile. "Yep, that's perfect. Now, when you swing the club, you want to keep your feet planted. When you swing the club follow the motion all the way through, don't stop as soon as you hit the ball." I guide her through the motions my father taught me. He really hoped I would like golf as much as he does, but I'm more of a hands-on guy. He stopped taking me to the course with him when he realized it wasn't my thing. "You ready to try it by yourself?"

"Yep." She stands with her feet shoulder width apart this time, shaking her arms out to loosen up. When she hits the ball, it flies to the left and not toward the targets in the field. If this were baseball it would definitely be a foul ball.

Disappointment washes over her. She's used to picking up on things quickly, and I don't want her to think one bad shot means she sucks. I place another ball on the short tee. "Here, try again."

Another wide shot, this time going right instead of left. "There's no use, I might as well give up now."

"It takes practice. It's okay if you don't get it right away...you aren't being tested over it."

She stomps her foot, and its actually kind of adorable. I can handle her glares and all out tantrums, but this isn't even close to those. A laugh escapes my lips and she glares at me. "This is why I never played sports in high school. I'm a geeky girl. I like to read, watch weird movies, and make sure I'm ready for the zombie apocalypse." She waves her hand in front of her face and body, "This was not made for sports of any kind. Even, golf."

She's staring the ball down as if it's her mortal enemy. "Why don't you shift your body a little bit? It should correct the direction of your swing."

"I guess," she huffs. "If I don't get it this time, I'm

done. I'm not going to keep letting myself fail over and over again. Not when I know it's a hopeless cause."

Darcy inhales then lets out a long slow breath. I've seen her do this so many times during her yoga sessions, and I know it's so she can center herself and focus. She squares her body, determination in her eyes. She lines the club up with the tiny ball, pulls her arms back and swings.

The ball doesn't go far, but at least it's straight ahead. Jumping up and down, she throws herself at me. Club still in hand she almost takes out one of the waitresses. I reach behind me, plucking the small metal rod from her hands. "You did it."

"I did," she exclaims. "I did it. How long do we still have in this booth?"

"About forty-five minutes."

"Good," she lets go of me turning back to the expanse of green covering the course. "I *will* hit one of those targets before our time is up."

"Have at it."

I want to take a few swings with the club, but Darcy is having fun and I'm not going to take that from her. She needs to allow some silliness into her life. If this is what makes her happy, and causes that smile on her face, I'll bring her here every fucking day. I'll do anything to keep her smiling.

I watch her take swing after swing, the ball going a bit further each time. When there's only five minutes left, she places another golf ball on the tee. "I'm going to do it this time," she smirks. "That target is mine."

I watch with trepidation as she swings the club and the ball hurls through the air. I hope she hits the stupid target. I forgot how competitive she can be, even if it's only against herself. I see the target in front of us light up as Darcy's ball hits it.

"I told you." She throws the club on the ground, doing this weird little dance number. "I told you I would do it this time."

"You sure did." I don't care how many people are around, or if they can see, I place my palms on her cheeks and lean in to kiss her. It escalates quickly and one of the servers taps my shoulder.

"Sir," he deadpans. "Your time is up."

I look to Darcy. "What do you say we play a friendly game of mini golf?"

"Sure," she shrugs. "As long as you're okay with losing."

"Whatever you say, Tiger."

We walk to the other side of the complex to have this showdown. I should have been better prepared. After the way she improved her driving skills, I know there isn't a chance in hell I will beat her. But seeing the pure joy she's exuding, I can't wait to tell Cami I made her "uptight" friend have the smallest iota of fun.

darcy

DERRICK and I have officially been dating for a little over a week. So far, we've managed to work out a schedule to see each other. Most mornings were both busy with him practicing and me working at the coffee shop, and I spend some of my evenings watching him practice. Like I'm doing right now, just so I can see him.

His dedication to basketball is admirable, and anyone watching him play can see how much he loves the sport. Tonight, he's working on his free throws. I think back to all those times I would watch him before I left for college and in some ways feel like we've gone back in time. But now, it's different because we have both changed with the most drastic change being me.

A small part of me feels like he could very well become tired of me and ditch me for good this time. I know that night wasn't his fault, but that doesn't get rid of the fear of not being wanted. It's an unwarranted fear, but Derrick was my first real boyfriend and that night affected me more than I think even he knows.

"Keep your mind on practice," Bentley says. His voice brings me out of my studies. It's cold and demanding, and I hate the way he talks to Derrick sometimes. When I glance at Derrick, his eyes are on me, and my lips turned up at the corners at the sight of him. If only I hadn't over reacted, think of how long we would have been together today. We may not have, though. We could have burned through our feelings for each other and crashed horribly.

So, maybe Bentley is justified in the way he talks to Derrick at times. Derrick rolls his eyes, salutes his mentor, and begins dribbling the ball again. I take a break from studying to watch him practice. Within five minutes he has looked in my direction no less than twenty times. Am I a distraction to him? This was one of the things I worried about when we decided to start dating. I don't want us to become distractions to each other. We each have our own goals and our own lives to lead, and I don't want that to become moot because we are a couple. Maybe I should stop coming to his practices so that he can focus on making the basketball team. My heart breaks a little at the thought of not coming to his practices because that's less time I'll have to see him, but in the end, I need to do what's best for him. Even if he doesn't realize it's what I'm doing.

Digging around in my backpack I find my head-phones and slip them on over my head. This is the only way I know of to keep myself from looking at him any time Bentley tries to pull Derrick's attention back to practice. Hoping that if I stop noticing the looks he shoots my way maybe he'll focus on the game and not on me.

I'm engrossed in my biology book, so much that I don't notice Derrick standing right in front of me until he lifts one side of my headphones from my ear. "You ready to get out of here? Or, are you gonna stay in this gym and study for the rest of the night?" I can hear the amusement in his voice, even if he tries to hide it.

"Oh," I startle. "I didn't realize you were already done with practice."

Only then do I notice the gym lights have dimmed and most of the area is hidden within shadows. All except for him. One of the few lights still on bathes him in an ethereal glow. He's sweaty but looks good enough to eat. Who would have ever thought athletes would be the thing that does it for this nerdy girl? That's not completely true, it's not all athletes. Just Derrick. He's looking at me as if I'm the most important thing in his world. Honestly, I feel like it. He puts me on a pedestal and makes sacrifices from sleep and practice to ensure he sees me. He's also never made fun of who I used to be, and am slowly letting out again, or the over-planner I am now. That is part of what makes him so attractive to me.

"So," he breaks into my thoughts. "Are you ready to go?"

I shake my head, pushing my thoughts of how lucky I am aside. "Yeah, let's get out of here." I shove all of my things into my backpack, not caring how they land but hoping I don't crease anything too badly. The zipper being pulled to close it reverberates loudly in the empty gym.

Before I even have a chance to lift the bag to my back, a hand swoops under the strap, pulling it out of my grasp. "Let me get that for you." He heaves it onto his back. "What in the hell do you have in here? Bricks?"

Rolling my eyes, I try to take it back. "No, it's called books." I put my hands on my hips when he won't relinquish the backpack. "You know those things you use to study with."

"I know what books are, smartass."

There's no point in trying to carry my own bag. He won't let me do it because he's too much of a gentleman. I'm not sure why I even bothered trying to get it back. I begin walking to the gym doors. "Better to be a smartass than a dumbass," I call over my shoulder with a wink.

Derrick jogs to catch up with me. The ease with which he does it amazes me. He just finished an almost two-hour practice session, is carrying his own bags and mine. Maybe I should add weightlifting to my yoga routine. I feel inadequate next to him when it comes to physical fitness.

His hand takes mine, and he sways his arm gently. "I don't feel like going back to my room, yet. Do you want to go somewhere?"

I sniff in his direction. "Shouldn't you take a shower? You kind of stink." I'm totally joking. I would go anywhere with him regardless of what he looks or *smells* like. But, he doesn't have to know that.

Unfortunately for me, he protests that thought by wrapping his arms around me, making sure to rub as much sweat as he can onto me. "Now, you stink, too." Gross. If this were anyone else, I'd jab them in the stomach.

But it's Derrick. His brand of humor is something I relate to and love about him. I freeze in his arms; did I just think the word love. No, I can't have feelings that deep for him. We haven't really seen each other in a year, and the one time I did wasn't exactly pleasant. I'll figure that out later. For now...I'll enjoy every moment we have together. "You're ridiculous."

"But you like it."

"Maybe just a smidge." Finally, he releases me. "Where do you want to go?"

"Roasted?"

I groan. It's not that I don't love the place, but I'm always there to work or study. It'd be nice to go anywhere else.

He sees the disappointment on my face. "Or we can hang out in your dorm room and order in?"

I like that idea much better. I'm a homebody and I'd prefer being in my own space as opposed to crowded around a bunch of people. "Sounds good."

We leave the gym behind us as we walk to my building. The evenings are finally starting to cool down, and I can almost feel a hint of Fall trying to break through. Our time will be even more limited if Derrick makes the basketball team. I'll do my best to take it day by day, but it's going to be hard.

I'm rushing around trying to pick up Cami's dirty laundry. One of these days she's going to learn how to put her clothes in the basket I have set up in the corner. One day she'll be grateful for me. She's asked me to help her stay organized countless times, does well for a few weeks, and falls off the wagon. I know Derrick has been subjected to Cami's messiness before, but I don't want it lying all around when me and him are hanging out. Luckily, he's on his phone and not paying attention to what I'm doing.

The springs of my mattress squeak lightly as he sits down in the center of my bed. He sets his phone down beside him and pats the space next to him. "The pizza is ordered, and I even got one with ham and pineapple on it just the way you like." He rubs his hand across his chin studying the room around us. "You know you don't have to clean up after her, right? She does the same crap in our dorm room and I've gotten used to it. You can't make a naturally scattered person into an organized person overnight."

"I know," I sigh. "But it's not just for your benefit. It literally makes me twitchy. I can't focus on anything when I'm surrounded by chaos."

He laughs, a lot harder than I think is warranted. Will he ever stop giving me grief over my overbearing tendencies? "I can see that." He pats the space next to him *again* because I still haven't sat down. "Forget about her mess, sit over here, and relax. We can put on a movie or something."

In the end I do as he asks. There's no point in arguing with him when I know he won't give up. But before walking to my bed, I dig around in the desk drawer trying to find the FireStick. It's not in the space where it's supposed to be and I check the television to see if it is still plugged in. I breathe a sigh of relief when I see it hooked up to the TV. I grab the remote from the desk, shocked that Cami actually put that back where it goes, and grateful I don't have to search for it.

"So, what do you want to watch?" I ask as I plop onto the bed next to Derrick.

He scoots to the far side and pulls me along with him until I'm nestled underneath his arm. "Whatever you want to watch. I'm game for anything."

"Really? Anything?"

He pulls me tighter against him. "Yep, anything." He pauses for a beat. "Except for those weird sci-fi movies you watch that involve ginormous animals that attack people."

Well, there goes watching *Sharknado*. Too bad, it's one of my guilty pleasure movies. I scroll through my watch list until I land on *Doctor Who*. A groan of frustration comes from the other side of my bed, and I can't help laughing. It's his fault he only specified weird animal sci-fi movies. He never said anything about a traveling time lord and his trusty companion. I don't even bother with the Ninth Doctor, everyone knows the Tenth is where all the awesome is.

Just as the opening credits begin there's a knock on the door. The smell coming from the hallway is delicious and I can't wait to dive into my pizza. Derrick bounces out of the bed before I even have a chance to get up. "I've got it."

After paying the delivery person and getting our pizza, he walks to the cabinet where we keep a few plates and utensils, pulls two of each out and comes back to the bed. "Why do you have forks?" I ask, perplexed.

"Um," he mumbles. "To eat with?"

"You don't eat pizza with a fork. That's sacrilege."

"Mom always made us eat it with a fork so we didn't make a mess." He shrugs his shoulders and his cheeks are bright. I might have embarrassed him a little. "So, unless you want glorious pizza stains on your comforter, you'll have to deal with me eating my pizza with a fork."

"Whatever floats your boat. It's not my place to judge." I grab the boxes from his hands so he can climb back in. I also grab a stack of napkins from my night-stand. I like to be prepared. But I also hate having to get back up to grab some when I forget. It's just easier to keep them here. Grabbing one, I unfold it until it's one flat surface, and tuck a corner into Derrick's collar. He lifts an eyebrow in question. "If you have to eat with a fork, I assume you also need a bib."

He shoves me, playfully, almost knocking me off the bed. "Smart ass."

"I think we've already had this conversation."

"Just turn the show back on." He replies, cutting into his pizza with the side of his fork. I can't stop the giggle from escaping my lips, and I'm given an eye roll in return.

"Look who wants to watch the *Doctor's* fascinating journeys all of a sudden."

He grabs the remote from where it lies on the bed, pressing the play button. "It's better than you giving me crap about eating with a fork."

"I agree." We eat in silence as we watch episode after episode of *Doctor Who*. Getting lost in the different worlds he takes us to and the people that need his help.

The door opening and closing awakens me. I didn't even realize I fell asleep. Cami whispers into the darkness, "Sorry, I didn't mean to wake you." Then she tiptoes to her bed and the soft rustle of sheets fill the room as she slides in.

"It's okay," I answer. Turning over, I roll into Derrick. I thought he would have left after I crashed on him, but he didn't. I'm not in a rush to kick him out of my dorm either. I wrap my arm around his waist, and he pulls me closer to snuggle. As hectic as my life is, I'm incredibly happy for these small moments of peace.

derrick

SOMEONE NUDGES me in the side and I jerk awake, hitting my knee on the underside of my desk. When I glance up, Darcy is staring at me. Shit, did I fall asleep in class again? Since Darcy has stopped coming to my practices Bentley has been keeping me there later and later. She told me the reason for her absence is that she's a distraction to me, but I still can't get my head fully in the game even when she's not there. I'm running on a lot less sleep while trying to juggle everything. This is the third class I've fallen asleep in this week, but at least I know Darcy will fill me in on what I miss. If only she could do that for every class.

Darcy mouths, "Are you okay?"

I nod, rubbing the sleep out of my eyes and trying to get my bearings. I feel everything but okay right now, I just don't want her to see how exhausted I truly am. I've never been this bone deep tired before and I'm not sure how to manage my time without upsetting someone. I can't skip out on any of my classes to get rest, obviously. And my time with Darcy is already limited because of the extra practice sessions. But, if I cut down on my practices there's a good chance I won't make the team. Or, at least that's what Bentley tells me. Tryouts are in a week and I need to make sure I have everything down so I don't make a fool of myself in front of the coaches.

The rest of the class goes by in a foggy haze. I'm not asleep... But I'm not actively paying attention either. I can't seem to focus enough to want to even acknowledge what we're learning. It would help if this professor had a little bit of life in his voice, maybe then I wouldn't be so prone to passing out during his lectures. His voice reminds me of the teacher in a movie my parents made me watch with them about a kid that skips school but never gets caught.

Darcy sidles up beside me and grabs my hand, pulling me toward the classroom door. "You look tired. Are you getting enough sleep at night?"

I'm not, but I'm not going to tell her that. By the time I finish up practice, then spend time with her, and scramble to get all my homework done, there's not much time for sleep. "Yeah," I shrug. "I guess it's just nerves about tryouts. I'm sure I'll be fine once they are finally over and I find out if I've made the team or not."

We walk out the front door of the building as she ponders my answer. I know she doesn't believe me but she's sweet enough that she won't call me out on it. I'm so happy she decided to give us another shot because I don't think I'd be handling the pressure without her. She grounds me in a way that I've never felt before.

The weather is finally starting to cool down and I'm grateful for it. I imagine all the things Darcy and I can do now that it's not hot as hell. The possibilities are endless. Maybe we can do another short camping trip, just the two of us. Hell, I may even set up the tent in record time. Or, maybe we just really need a date night. We spend so many nights in either her dorm or mine, eating takeout and watching movies. I think it's time to shake it up a little. I don't want her to get bored or tired of me falling asleep during some of the shows she watches. But mostly the bored thing. I can't have her thinking this is what a forever with me will look like. If she even wants me that long.

We're halfway across the lawn when I pull her to a stop and wrap my arms around her. "Do you have any plans tonight?"

"Um, not that I know of." She giggles completely taken off guard by my sudden shift in mood.

"You don't have to work tonight?"

"Nope," she pops the "p" with more exaggeration than usual. "I opened the shop this morning, so I'm off tonight and tomorrow morning." Her arms wrapped around my waist and she nestles deeper into my chest. "Why? What do you want to do? I'm sure I can find something on Netflix that we can watch."

I scoff. "Is that our new normal? Netflix and chill?"

"Well, technically we are just hanging out. Not the other meaning of chill."

"I wasn't implying otherwise." I kiss her forehead before twirling her around. "But, that's not what I had in mind. I want to take you out."

"Where?" She scrunches up her nose, not very excited about the idea.

"Don't you worry about that." I bring her in for a kiss. "Just be ready when I get to your dorm at seven." I turn toward the gym, needing to find Bentley so I can cancel practice tonight. "Just an FYI, tonight is going to be a fancy date," I call over my shoulder.

When I look back, she's staring at me as if I've grown another head. Good. That's exactly what I want. Unexpected fun is always a good thing. I just need to figure out what sort of fancy date I'm going to take her on.

Bentley was less than thrilled with my announcement about missing practice tonight. I have to make it up by being in the gym insanely early in the morning. There goes my hope of getting any sleep tonight. A small pit of worry forms in my stomach at the mere thought that this could impact my chance of making the team, but it all drains away when Darcy opens the door.

She's wearing a slinky black dress that barely meets the middle of her thighs, leaving the rest of her smooth skin on display. Her long blonde hair, which is usually pulled up in a bun of some sort, hangs in loose curls over her shoulders. It takes everything in me to not reach out and run my fingers through the soft waves. She's even wearing makeup. The most I've ever seen her wear is lip-gloss and maybe a little mascara. Bright red lipstick finishes the look and pulls it together.

She stands in the doorway rubbing her hands together, clearly uncomfortable even though she shouldn't be. "Do you want to come in?" Her voice is barely above a whisper, and I have to lean in to hear her.

What I mean to say is yes, but that's not what comes out. "You are breathtaking." When she doesn't say anything, I continue. "I mean it. You look stunning."

"Oh, thank you." She twirls a strand of hair around her finger and opens the door wider for me to enter. "I just need to grab my bag then we can go."

"No problem, take your time." I don't even recognize the room right now. There are clothes and shoes strewn about, and I'm shocked Darcy isn't running around to straighten it up. I can't believe she's the cause of this mess, but I will say that it was all worth it. Hell, I'll offer to come clean her room tomorrow to show my appreciation.

Cami is sitting on Darcy's bed smiling from ear to ear. No doubt proud of Darcy for stepping out of her comfort zone. And, if I had to guess, she was most likely in charge of this transformation. It has her signature written all over it.

She studies me from head to toe, taking in what I'm

wearing. It's nothing too dressy, but it's a nice pair of slacks and a button up shirt. I can't very well tell Darcy to dress up, then show up like a slob. "You better treat her right tonight, Rhodes."

Rhodes? She has never called me by my last name, I wonder what changed. "Um, I think you mean Derrick?" I scratch the back of my neck, unsure of how Cami is going to respond.

"Nope, I mean Rhodes."

"Why?"

"Because... Now, you're actually dating my best friend, and it's my duty to defend her honor. You break her heart, I'll break your face." She curls one hand into a fist then slams it into her palm, demonstrating her threat.

My hands go up in surrender. "Calm down, killer. I'm not going to break her heart." I hold out my hand in a peace offering. "I also think it's partly my job to defend her honor."

"Yeah, but it will always be sisters before misters." She takes my hand with a firm grasp and shakes it. "I'll be keeping an eye on you."

"Okay..." This got weird really fast.

"Cami," Darcy calls from the closet. "You are so full of crap. Stop scaring him, please."

Cami bursts into a fit of laughter. "Why did you have to ruin the moment? I had him fooled for a minute."

"You weren't serious?"

"No," she chokes on a laugh. "I wasn't serious. I'm not a bitch."

"I thought it was kind of weird that you doing the good cop/bad cop thing. It's very unlike you." I glance at my watch. What in the world is taking her so long to grab a purse? She said it would only take a minute, it's been almost five.

"Eh," she shrugs, now under control. "I wanted to have a little fun. Consider it payback for ratting me out as part of the plan for camping."

"I wasn't going down in flames on my own."

Darcy walks out of the closet with a *Doctor Who* bag slung across her body, trying to hide it behind her back. It took her that long for *that* bag?

"Woah, girl," Cami jumps off the bed. "What the hell is that?" She's pointing at the bag as if it's existence offends her.

"It's my bag," Darcy deadpans.

"Why didn't you use one of mine?" She points toward the closet. "There are a ton in there. He said *fancy*, and that my friend is not fancy."

"She's fine, Cami," I interrupt before she says something to hurt Darcy's feelings. I can understand why she changed her entire persona when she came to college. I guess it isn't easy being nerdy and having fandoms. "She could be dressed in sweatpants and I would still think she's the most beautiful girl in the room."

"I guess," Cami mutters.

But my attention isn't on her. It's on the girl with the

huge grin and rosy cheeks. I walk to her and pull her into my chest. "Are you ready to go?" I whisper into her ear.

"Yep." She nods. "I'll be home later, Cam."

Cami not so discreetly winks. "Don't do anything I wouldn't do."

I roll my eyes. That girl is a hot mess. But she has Darcy's best interests at heart and is a pretty awesome girlfriend to Travis.

Grabbing Darcy's hand, I pull her toward the door and to what I hope will be a romantic evening. Hopefully she'll like what I have planned for the evening.

darcy

"WHERE ARE WE GOING?" I'm second guessing my decision to wear heels. If I'd known we'd be walking to our destination, I would have opted for flats.

"It's not much further." He stops, and I almost run into his back. Turning around he bends down, lifting one of my feet in his hands. "Do you want me to take your shoes off? I know they can't be comfortable."

While walking barefoot would definitely keep blisters from forming, I'm not excited about walking on the damp grass with no shoes. Imagine all the germs, bleh. He takes my silence as refusal, and it is. "The other option is a piggyback ride."

"It'd almost be safer for me to walk barefoot." I take note of the length of my dress, which isn't very long at all. Damn Cami for picking this one out. It's impractical. "I'm positive if I climbed on your back, I'd be flashing anyone who walks by."

He smirks at me before standing. "So, you'd rather kill your feet than any of my suggestions?"

"Your ideas aren't that great at this moment." I deadpan. "You said fancy. I assumed we'd be going somewhere in a vehicle... Not walking across campus."

He pulls me closer to him and puts his arm around my back. Before I even know what is happening, he swoops his other arm underneath my leg and cradles me in his arms. "This is option three." He bounces gently, adjusting his grip on me. "The whole fancy thing was to see what you would wear."

I wrap my arms around his neck, ensuring I won't fall if he can't hold my weight. "Oh yeah? Did I meet your expectations?"

His head bends just enough that he can kiss my forehead. "Yep. You blew my expectations out of the water."

"Well, I didn't do it on my own. You should probably thank Cami." Feeling embarrassed about being carried like a baby, I burrow further into his chest. He smells divine. A mixture of cologne and soap. The same way he smelled when he would hold me close as we watched movies. How was that only a year ago?

Instead of replying, he comes to a stop and whispers, "We're here." He lowers me to the ground, slowly. I'm facing him and he nods at something, or someone, behind me. "Do you want to turn around?"

I'm not sure if I do or not. This night isn't going at all the way I expected. Not necessarily in a bad way. It's just *different*. He's showing me an entirely different side of him. One that I have no doubt I'll fall head over heels for.

His happy smile begins to fade. The corners of his mouth dipping down. Dang, I don't want him thinking I don't appreciate whatever he's put together for the night. I do, and I'm thrilled he's putting so much effort into dating me. Especially when we haven't been able to see each other as much. I'm not even sure what's holding me back right now. Fear of what the future might hold is definitely one of the things, but other than that I can't really say.

My promise to take things moment by moment with him rushes to the forefront of my brain. There's no need to worry about what *might* happen later on down the road. I have this moment, right now, with him. I close my eyes, inhale deeply, and turn around.

My exhale releases in a whoosh. How much thought did he put into this? When he asked me if I had plans, he made it seem like we were going to some sort of restaurant. Like it was a request on a whim. This definitely wasn't what I expected.

We are in the quad close to Derrick's building. I don't know why I didn't register the location sooner, but I guess I was too wrapped up in my own thoughts. There's a table covered with a white tablecloth and a setting for two across from each other. Flameless candles are dotted along the surface, brightening up the area. There are even blankets spread across the bench seats to keep our clothes from being ruined. I may end up using one to keep warm. I didn't bring a sweater and the air has gotten cooler than it was earlier.

Derrick stands behind me and places his hands on my hips. Thumbs rubbing back and forth right above my hip bone. "Do you like it?" His voice holds uncertainty as he whispers in my ear.

I grab his hands, pulling them around me. Letting myself sink into his embrace. "I love it."

This is more than anyone has ever done for me. Not that I have much experience since Derrick has been the first and only guy I've ever seriously dated, but he freaking nailed it. I didn't think guys put this much thought into dates anymore. It seems like most people just hang out. That's fine and all since I'm a self-proclaimed home body, but it feels amazing to be dazzled. To know that I'm worth this much effort.

He squeezes me tight for a couple of beats, then releases me. Grabbing my hand, he pulls me toward the table. "I hope you're hungry."

It's then that I see the shadow of some sort of basket sitting on one of the benches. As we get closer, the smell of pasta sauce permeates the air, and my stomach grumbles, disrupting the silence. "I could eat," I wince. "How in the world did you pull this off in such a short amount of time?"

"I had some help." He grins, and he's never looked as handsome as he does now. Don't get me wrong, he is good looking even on his worst days. But now, the way the moonlight shines down on him, he looks ethereal. Almost too good to be true.

"You aren't going to tell me?"

"Nope, but only because I'm sure you already know who helped me."

Cami and Travis to the rescue once again. "Oh yeah?" I quirk my eyebrow. Grateful that they care so much about Derrick and I making it as a couple, but also frustrated that he seems to need their help at every turn.

He's setting all the food out, but stills at the tone of my voice. "Yeah." He pauses, no doubt gauging my sudden irritation. "I needed Travis to make sure nobody took this spot, or the food, while I went to get you."

"Oh." Gah, I'm such a crappy person for assuming they helped come up with the idea for this date. Derrick is perfectly capable of thinking up interesting dates on his own. I mean he did take me to that golf park. I know for a fact Cami would never suggest something like that.

"What's wrong, Dar?" The smile he so proudly wore moments ago falters. "Is this not okay?"

"No," I rush the words out. I don't want him to think I don't appreciate everything he's done tonight. "I just thought Travis and Cami planned this date for us." Shrugging, I sink into myself. Ashamed of even thinking that. "I felt like maybe you were relying on them too much for our dates, and that you weren't putting in as much effort as I thought."

The ground has suddenly become fascinating. My toes garnering all my attention so I can't see the disappointment that has to be written all over Derrick's face. This is what happens when my insecurities creep up on me... I say, and do, things that ruin everything.

Derrick's strong arms encircle me, pulling me close to him. "I only needed their help with ideas for camping. It was the only way I could think of to get you to talk to me for more than five seconds. And ensure you wouldn't run away when I brought up a possibility of us." He bends down, until he's almost squatting, and grabs my hands. His eyes are on mine when he begins speaking again. "Everything else has been all me. I would do anything for you. Even order your favorite food and dessert so we can have a nice, romantic dinner alone."

"I know." I tug his hands, wanting him to get back up. He shouldn't be the one explaining himself to me. "I'm sorry," I say as a tear slides down my cheek. Not from sadness, but overwhelming joy that I mean that much to him. "I don't know what is wrong with me. I always say the wrong things. How are you even still interested in me?"

I look up at him, and all I see is adoration. "Because," he whispers into the stillness surrounding us. "You are the only person I've wanted since last summer. You have to know that by now."

"I do," I say quietly. "I just might need a reminder from time to time."

"I'll remind you as long as you'll have me." He leans in, brushing his lips across mine. His tongue caresses the seam of my lips, asking permission. My mouth parts and the kiss deepens. My fingers grasp the front of his shirt, pulling him closer, until there isn't an inch of space between us.

We are lost in each other, and I savor this moment. Knowing it won't be the last. A voice yells from somewhere above us, "Get a room."

I pull away from him, embarrassed at being caught making out in public. Not that I'm ashamed, it's just not something I usually do. But he tends to make me throw caution to the wind. He brings out the best in me and comforts me when my insecurities come out in full force.

"Mind your own business," Derrick shouts back. Smirking, he grabs my hand. "We should eat. The food is going to get cold."

I groan after I finish the last of the spaghetti on my plate. I was hungrier than I thought. I've never been able to finish an entire helping of spaghetti, but tonight, it didn't stand a chance.

After putting my plate beside the basket, I walk around the table and sit next to Derrick. The temperature keeps dropping, and I need warmth. This dress isn't made for evening dinners in the quad. He puts his arm around my shoulder and grabs the end of the blanket covering the bench to cover my legs. My head settles onto his shoulder, listening to the breeze rattle the leaves on the trees.

"I hope you have room for dessert."

"Not likely," I pat my stomach. "I don't think I can fit any more food into my body."

"I'll get all of this cleaned up, and then I'll walk you back to your dorm." He pulls away but takes the part of the blanket he was sitting on and drapes it over me.

I watch him as he quickly, but carefully, arranges the dishes and table decorations inside the basket. Plates stacked on top of each other on one side of the takeout bag, while the tablecloth, candles and extra blanket are placed on the other, ensuring the dirty dishes won't get anything else messy.

I stand up as soon as he's finished, wrapping the blanket tightly around me like a cloak. "Do you need me to carry anything?"

"No, I've got it." He glances at my feet, still in the heels Cami let me borrow. "Unless I need to carry you so that your feet don't hurt. I can come back and get this later."

I carefully pull the heels off, putting them in one hand. I don't want to walk barefoot, but I'll do it so he doesn't have to make two trips. "I'm good." I wave the offending shoes at him.

"Do you mind if we stop by my room and drop this off?"

"Not at all."

The walk to his dorm building is quiet. The soft sounds of music and conversation drifting from rooms we pass along the way are the soundtrack to the end of our date. I'm not ready to go home just yet, but I don't want to invite myself to stay, either.

I open the door of his building and a blast of cool air hits me in the face. Why do these people still have the air conditioner down so low? Burrowing further into the blanket I follow Derrick to the elevator bank.

We don't have to wait long after I press the button before the doors slide open. He awkwardly gestures for me to go before him. As soon as the doors are closed I ask, "Where's Travis tonight?"

"I'm not sure. I think he had to tutor someone then he was going to hang out with Cami." He glances at me out of the corner of his eye. "Why?"

"Just wondering," I rock back and forth on my feet. Nervous about being alone with him in his room, even if it's only for a few moments. We've been in my room without an audience, but it's different. It's my personal space, and I have control there. I'm able to set boundaries.

Travis is nowhere in sight when we walk into their dorm room. And, his room is much cleaner than the way I left mine. I really hope Cami cleaned it up some before she met up with Travis. If not, I'm going to have to rush to get it all done before classes in the morning. Or, do it tonight before I go to bed. I'm not a fan of either option. I slide the blanket off my shoulders and place it on his unmade bed.

Derrick pulls the paper bag out of the basket before setting it under the desk that houses their TV. He slides the chair in front of it, and to my skeptical gaze he shrugs. "I'll get it cleaned up after I take you home." His gaze roves over my body again, with more heat than earlier. "Unless, you aren't ready to go home yet?"

He questions rather than states, giving me control over how the rest of the night will play out. "I think I want to stay." I walk closer to him. Unsure of where to put my hands, I settle them around his neck. Being flirty is definitely not my thing. I don't know what I'm supposed to do or say. I feel absolutely ridiculous standing like this. "I mean, I want to stay."

"Are you sure?" He studies me for any hint of indecision.

He won't find any. I *want* to be here with him. "I'm sure. We're always at my dorm, it's nice to be away for a little bit without worrying about Cami barging in."

"Okay," he nods. "Do you want to watch a movie or something? We can eat the dessert I got before it's ruined."

"That sounds great."

"Anything you want to watch in particular?"

"Nope, I'm good with whatever you choose." I look down at the dress, and don't want to lie down in it. "Um, do you have anything I can change into? Watching movies in this isn't going to be very comfortable."

"Yeah," he goes through his drawers searching for something for me to wear. It's as if he's looking for something in particular.

I laugh when he pulls out clothes that actually belong to me. "Where in the world did you get these?"

"You left them at my house after we went swimming. I held on to them just in case."

"So, you predicted that I would need these clothes from you in the future." I take the Thor t-shirt and yoga pants from his hands. "Pretty presumptuous of you, don't you think?"

"Eh," he closes the drawer. "I would have just kept them if things didn't work out in my favor."

"That's heading into creepy territory."

He stands taller, crossing his arms. "Let's just say I have faith in myself and knew you would need them one day."

"If you say so." I walk to his closet and turn on the light before closing the door. "I'll be right out."

I hear the television come on… and foil, or something similar, being torn open. God, I hope that's not what I think it is. While I'm certain I'll cross that path with him in the future, tonight is not that night.

I'm relieved when I walk out of the closet and there are two containers holding tiramisu on the bed. Climbing on the bed, I'm careful not to knock them over. Derrick presses play before I even register what's on the screen.

I look over at him in shock. "You're okay with watching *The Walking Dead*? I thought you hated this show."

"I do, but you like it, so I'll watch it."

"Aw, you're so sweet." I bat my lashes at him. "Letting me watch carnage instead of whatever you wanted to watch."

"I didn't think you'd like watching sports recaps."

I scrunch up my nose. "You would be correct."

We eat the tiramisu while watching Daryl battle the undead. It's not the best thing to watch while eating, but it doesn't faze me.

Before long, Derrick is snoring softly beside me. I move the containers to the desk and snuggle up next to him. I could go home, but I don't want to. I like waking up next to him. Being the first and last thing he sees in a day isn't all that bad, either.

derrick

THE UNEVEN SOUND of balls being dribbled on the court is enough to give anyone a headache. Basketball tryouts are today, and I'm more nervous than I thought I would be. I didn't anticipate the amount of people that wanted to be a part of the Hilltown basketball team. Not only that, but there are also students sitting in the stands to watch us.

It definitely isn't helping my state of mind. The ball in my hand becomes damp with sweat. There is no way I'm going to make the team if I don't get my shit under control.

"Everyone, line up." Coach Wade, the head basketball coach, yells from the center of the court. "This is how tryouts are going to work. I'm going to count you out into groups of five, and then we will run through some drills. After that, each group will scrimmage against each other. This is to give us an idea of how you work as a team." His legs are hip width apart and his arms are crossed over his wide chest as if he is some sort of surly bodyguard. "Any questions?"

I assume everyone shakes their head no because Coach starts at one end of the line and counts off potential players until there is a total of five teams. I take a quick look into the stands to see if Darcy has made it before joining my temporary teammates by one of the goals. She hasn't shown up yet. I wonder if it's because she thinks she'll be a distraction. That couldn't be further from the truth. Her being here would help more than hurt.

The guys I'm paired with are huge. How in the hell am I going to shine compared to them? I'm not even sure if the coach will be able to see me behind their shadows. I wish Darcy were here to help give me the confidence boost I need right now.

The drills are fairly easy, but I'm glad I worked so hard with Bentley. Those early morning and late-night practices have paid off. While the guys I'm paired with are good, the edge I have from my time with Bentley puts me slightly above them. Seeing the caliber of the players I am up against, to make the team, makes me appreciate how hard he was on me leading up to this moment.

Coach Wade and the assistant coaches are making their way around the gym, studying each player for a short amount of time. When they get to my group, we are working on our three-pointers. This is the main thing I've been working with Bentley on because even though

I'm strong in other areas, I feel like my height has always been a hindrance with this shot. As the ball leaves my hands I notice Coach staring in my direction, and I hope with every fiber of my being that I make this shot. The faint swish of the net hits my ears, and when Coach nods his head the tiniest bit, my shoulders sag in relief.

It's safe to say I gained his approval, and if not that, then definitely his attention. I've been watching him make his rounds, and he hasn't been showing any sort of emotion unless he finds the player adequate. The way he studies our movements and actions is almost robotic, and it's kind of scary how detached he is. I'm going to have to wow him during the scrimmages. Maybe I'll get lucky and be on the team that has to go twice.

"Everybody, listen up." Wade's booming voice has everyone grabbing their basketballs and going silent. Even the students in the stands have quieted their chatter. It is shocking how commanding his voice is, and I know playing under him will make me better play but will also be difficult. "I want everyone to stay with your group and sit on the first row of the stands."

It's a mad dash to get to our seats as quickly as possible. Nobody wants to disappoint the coach. As soon as everyone is seated he begins talking. "I'm impressed with what I saw during drills, but now is when it's really going to matter." He points at the groups closest to the home entrance. "You are team one and team two. We are going to do twenty-minute scrimmages with ten minute halves. From the first four teams that play, I will pick five people to play the last team." He takes a moment to make sure we all understand what he's saying. He'll pick the five guys that stand out. "Team one and two, get on the court. Teams three and four, be ready when this game is over."

I'm on the third team, so I have at least twenty minutes to psych myself up. As the game gets underway, I can already tell who isn't going to make the cut. It's not that they're bad, but they aren't ready to be playing at this level. I only hope Coach Wade finds me worthy of a position on his team.

It's finally my team's turn to go and saying the five of us are nervous is an enormous understatement. During the last game, my teammates and I discussed a few plays we could maneuver against the other team. Those tactics may not work once we are in the heat of the game, but at least we are all on the same page and won't be running around like chickens with their heads cut off. I have to make sure the coaches notice me. I can't fail at this point. I've sacrificed too much time to not make the team. Hell, I've lost hours of sleep and fallen behind in some of my classes. I *need* to make the team.

The people in the stands watching us try out are a dull background noise. I've completely drown them out and all I hear are sneakers squeaking on the shiny hardwood floor. I'm in my element. My group is working well together...mostly. Two of the guys keep missing passes and causing turnovers. I can tell the others are getting frustrated, but there isn't much we can do about it.

Our scrimmage is almost over when I spot Darcy standing in the doorway to the gym. She's leaning against the open door, bag at her feet, and eyes on me. She made it. Has she been watching the entire time? I turn my attention back to the game. We're down by two points. That last turnover put the other guys ahead. I am *not* losing this scrimmage.

I dart around the guy defending me and come to the other side. The ball comes barreling at me. I glance down, dribbling the ball once, twice, and line up my shot. I'm right outside the threepoint line. If I make this we win the scrimmage. A glance at the clock shows seconds left in the game. I jump up, releasing the ball at the same time. The buzzer goes off, and the ball goes through the goal. Nothing but net. We won the scrimmage.

My teammates gather around me, slapping me on the back, talking about that last shot, and how they were worried we were going to lose. I block their chatter out and look around them. Darcy is clapping and wearing the biggest smile. It lights up her eyes, and I'm happy that I've made her proud.

We take our seats in the stands while the coaches hold a small meeting in the center of the court, going over notes they took during the scrimmages. Wade and one of the assistant coaches look over at me and return back to their debate.

The wait feels like an eternity but is really only a few minutes. The coaches fan out on either side of Coach

Wade. A united front as they prepare to announce who is going to scrimmage the last team.

Wade doesn't bother with any sort of speech, he just calls out names. "Palmer, Alvarado, Barnes, Lambert, and Rhodes, you're scrimmaging the last team."

Shock keeps me rooted to my seat. When I wasn't in the first few names he called, I was sure he wasn't going to call me. Barnes, one of the guys on my team, slaps me on the back. "We should get out there."

The game goes by in a blur. Barnes and I play well with each other, and I hope we both make it. They are only taking on eight players, and since Coach chose us to play again, I can't help but think that the both of us have a spot on this team.

The five of us beat the last team and it feels amazing. Adrenaline rushes through me at the victory. It may be an inconsequential game to others, but for me it means making it or walking away from the sport I love. I've lived and breathed basketball for as long as I can remember, and I'll be crushed if this doesn't pan out the way I'm hoping.

Coach Wade stands on the sidelines with his clipboard in hand. "Gather 'round." He looks at the notes he's made, and we're all moving restlessly trying to hide what we're feeling. Fear, frustration, confidence, hope...I see it pass across everyone's faces. I'm sure my face mirrors theirs. Finally, he speaks, "That's it for tryouts today. We'll post a list of those that made the team on the door outside of the gym first thing in the morning.

We'll also send out an email if you've made the team, shortly after. We begin practicing next week." He hands the clipboard off to one of the other coaches. "You all did great out there. Even if you don't make the team this year, don't give up. Hone your skills and come back to tryout next year."

He turns and walks off without saying another word. Small groups form beside me, the team hopefuls discussing what they could have done better and speculating if they've made the team. My focus is on Darcy.

The students that watched us are filing out of the gym, bored now that the excitement is over. I weave through them until I finally reach Darcy. She doesn't hesitate. She jumps at me, arms around my neck and legs wrapped around my waist. Treating me like a champion before we even know if I've made the team. "You did amazing out there."

"You really think so?"

"I know so," she clings to me tighter. Then she slides down until her feet touch the ground, but her arms don't leave my neck. "Did you not see how the coaches were watching you? They'd be crazy not to take you on."

"I was a little busy playing ball to notice the coaches." I walk us toward the wall outside of the gym. We're blocking the exit and getting rude looks from everyone trying to leave. Her back ends up against the wall, and I move in closer to give us a little bit of privacy.

"Ah, you were too busy to watch the coaches. But you weren't too busy to search for me?" She leans up, placing a kiss along my jawline. She's starting to loosen up around me, and it sends a jolt of happiness through me. I didn't think she'd ever get to a point where she'd do more than hold my hand in front of other people.

"You're more important." I nuzzle her neck, and her skin warms with the blush I'm sure is turning her cheeks red. "Want to get out of here?"

She nods her agreement and I pull away. "What do you want to do?"

"I don't know. Sleep?" I laugh. "I'm good with anything as long as I can do it sitting down. That was exhausting." She's picking her bag up from the floor and throws it over her shoulder. "Let me go grab my phone and we can head out."

"Sounds good." She passes the last few stragglers in the gym, mostly likely friends of some of the guys that tried out and takes a seat in one of the chairs. "I'll be right here waiting."

Jogging toward the locker room, I think about how tryouts went. They were better than expected, and I do hope my name is on that list in the morning. But, even if I don't make it, I'll just try out again next year. All that matters right now is getting out of these sweaty clothes and hanging out with my girl.

darcy

I THOUGHT my time with Derrick was short when he was practicing with Bentley. But, it's nothing compared to his new schedule as part of the team. I'm beyond proud of him for making the team, but we rarely have any sort of valuable time together.

It's especially frustrating now that I have more hours away from the coffee shop. Tom hired even more people to take some of the burden off of Cami and me. We were there almost every day, and it begins to take its toll. I'm relieved to have the extra time for myself, but I don't know how to fill it. There's more time for comic books and fangirling over my favorite shows, but I need another hobby.

Or, I need my boyfriend around so I have someone to hang out with. Cami has been busy with classes, and Travis, leaving me to entertain myself most days. When did I become so needy? I was fine being a loner when I was in high school. Hell, I didn't really have any friends when I came to Hilltown. Not until, Cami asked me to go to a party with her.

The door swings open, almost hitting the wall. Speak of the devil. "Where's the fire?" I call out as she throws her bag on the bed.

She jumps and whips around. "You scared the shit out of me."

Laughing, I shrug, "I live here, too. At least, last time I checked, I did." When she doesn't give me a sarcastic reply, my brows furrow. She's usually on her A game with comebacks. "What's wrong?"

"This damn teacher is trying to flunk me out of the class." She kicks the side of her bed in frustration. "We aren't even halfway into the semester and I'm going to lose my scholarship."

"Take a deep breath, girl." She's in full on panic mode, and it's hard to calm her down when she's this upset. At least she won't go on benders anymore to deal with her emotions. I don't think she will anyway. "What class is it? Maybe I can help."

"I'm going to have to go to my father for help. I've done so well without him, I don't want to be back under his thumb." She's mumbling to herself, already going to the worst possible scenario.

I've got to do something. I can't let her go back to the unhappy wreck she was when she relied completely on her father. He wouldn't let her make any decisions for herself. It was his way or no way. She is not going back down that road. I'll do everything in my power to help her where she needs it.

I'm across the room in the next breath. Placing my hand on her shoulder, I turn her toward me. She has tears streaming down her face. "Cami, what class are you having problems with?"

"Does it matter? I don't understand anything about it. It makes no sense to me."

"It matters to me. I can help you." I pause, seeing the fear of what will happen if she calls her dad. "You don't have to call *him*. We may be different majors but we still have to take the same basics."

"You're right." She sighs. "Calling my father is the last thing I want to do." Her fingers run along her forehead, trying to rub out the tension she's feeling. "It's my economics class. I don't understand half of what we've covered."

"Why didn't you ask for help earlier? You know I would have helped you."

"I know. But, I got caught up in trying to get you and Derrick together, and I didn't want to bother you with it. Not when you were struggling with your feelings over him." She scans the room. "Where is he anyway? I figured you would be hanging out or something."

I groan in frustration. "Basketball practice. It's where he always is. I haven't spent any quality time with him in weeks. And it's only going to get worse when the season starts." I shake the depressing thoughts from my head.

"But, the plus side is I'll be able to help you ace this class."

"I don't think that's possible."

"Sure it is. We can do this." An idea hits me. One that I know she'll be totally on board with. "How about this? For each chapter we go over, and you successfully learn, we'll binge watch a season of *Buffy*."

"Do I get a gold star, too?" She deadpans.

"If it will make you happy, then yes."

"Fine. We'll try it your way. We haven't watched it in weeks."

Scrunching up my nose, I ask, "Do you think we'll ever get tired of that show?"

"Maybe. But it definitely makes our days better. I mean, if she can take on evil and pass her classes, surely I can get my shit together and tackle this class."

"There's the optimist I knew was lurking beneath the surface."

"Shut up," she lightly shoves me. "Be prepared for a billion questions. You offered, and you can't back out now."

"Grab your books. We'll work on it on my bed." I stare at the crumpled blankets and clothes scattered on her bed. "It's a cleaner workspace."

She flips me off before digging through her bag for her books. It may not be how I envisioned spending my evening, but it's totally worth it if she doesn't have to worry about her dad.

* * *

Cami and I are curled up on my bed watching *Buffy*. She finally has the first section in her economics class down. She just needed someone to explain it to her in a way she understands. Instead of starting the season from the beginning, we picked up where we left off last time. I'm proud of her for putting in the effort to learn the subject rather than call her dad and bow down to his will. She'll never go back down that road again if I have anything to do with it.

There's a knock on the door. It's soft and hesitant, as if person on the other side of the door is worried about disturbing us, or that we won't answer. Cami peers at the clock, "It's already eleven o'clock. Are you expecting anybody?"

"Not that I know of." The conversation is so close to the one we had when Derrick brought my yoga mat back to me.

"Well, I know it's not Travis. He texted me before he went to sleep over an hour ago." She taps her finger on her chin, "Maybe it's Derrick?"

"I don't see why he would be here. He doesn't usually come over after basketball practice."

Another knock sounds against the door. Cami climbs over me to get off the bed. "I'll see who it is."

She picks up the bat I bought her as an early birthday gift and holds it behind her back. Opening the door, she sighs in relief. "Oh, it *is* you."

A familiar voice laughs from the hallway, "You know you're not hiding that bat very well, don't you? If someone was here to harm you, they'd be able to disable you in no time."

"You don't have to be a jerk about it. At least I have some sort of protection if some weirdo tries to come into our dorm room. Besides," she flips her ponytail. "I can be scrappy if I have to."

"Can I come in?" His voice is low and sounds tired. He probably hasn't gotten much sleep since he's started basketball practice on top of his school work.

"Sure," Cami sets the bat on her bed and grabs her backpack. "I'll just, um, go downstairs and study some more."

I grab the remote from the nightstand, pause the DVD, and sit up straighter. Pulling my legs in to sit cross legged, I make room for Derrick to sit down. Cami is already out the door and shuts it with a soft click.

"Hi," I whisper. I'm not sure why he's here. He usually texts, or calls, when he gets home from practice. I should have known something was up when I didn't hear from him. A pit of worry builds up in my stomach, and I fear he is here with bad news. It wouldn't be surprising considering how little of him I've seen the past few weeks. I'm starting to feel like maybe I'm not as important to him as I thought I was.

He sets his duffel bag on the floor at the foot of my bed. Surely it can't be all bad if he is planning to stay.

"Hey," he crawls up my bed taking the spot Cami vacated only moments ago.

"I wasn't expecting you to come over tonight." My fingers begin twirling my hair of their own accord. "I mean it's not that I'm not happy you're here, but it's unexpected."

He pulls me close to him and wraps his arm around me. "I know, I just needed to see you. It feels like I haven't seen you in ages."

I know exactly what he means. I feel the same exact way, and that each day is pulling us further and further from each other. But I don't say anything. I'm not the type to do guilt trips. He's doing the best he can right now. When things calm down, it'll be easier. At least, that's what I keep telling myself.

"Agreed," I lean into him. "Are you staying tonight?"

"If you'll let me. Maybe we can start a movie." His voice is muffled in my hair, and the movement causes the strands that are down to tickle my neck.

I giggle. Being ridiculously ticklish is one of my fatal flaws, and he pokes me in the side to making me laugh harder. "Well, I'm not going to kick you out." I stare him down. "Unless, you keep tickling me."

"Okay, I'll stop the torture. Put on whatever you want, but I'm not making any promises that I'll make it all the way through it."

"Let me text Cami and let her know you're staying. I don't want her to be surprised when she comes back up and you're still here."

Darcy: Derrick is staying.
Cami: Cool. I'll go to their dorm. I have a key, and Travis will be surprised when he wakes up and I'm there.
Darcy: Text me when you get over there. Do you need anything?
Cami: Nope, I've got some clothes there.
Darcy: Don't forget to text me as soon as you're in the building.
Cami: Yes, Mom.

"Smartass," I mumble under my breath.

"Who?"

"Cami, she's going to stay in your room tonight."

"Cool."

I roll over to face to him, taking in the bags under his eyes. He really needs to sleep more. He's not going to be able to go on like this the whole semester. "So... *Marvel* or *DC*?"

"What?" His eyebrows arch in confusion.

"Which superheroes do you want to watch?"

"Oh," he says, running his fingertips along my arms. Goosebumps prickle my skin he's just touched. "*Marvel.*"

"Good choice."

We are halfway into *Avengers* when Derrick's eyes begin to close. I know I should let him sleep. He needs it way more than I do, and we have classes tomorrow. But, I don't want my time with him to end, yet. "Hey," I nudge him with my elbow.

His eyes snap open. "Yeah?"

"Which universe do you like better? *Marvel* or *DC*?"

"*Marvel*, obviously. But I like *DC*, too. Why?"

I pull the blanket tighter against us. It gets cold in this room, and I like snuggling beneath the covers next to my guy. "Just wondering." I pause for a moment, thinking of another question to ask so he'll keep his eyes open a little bit longer. "Do you consider Batman a superhero?"

"Yeah, I guess." He sighs. "He saves people just like all the other superheroes do. And if he wasn't then why would the creators group him in with the rest?"

"Just when I thought you were an okay guy." I shake my head in mock embarrassment.

"You don't think he's a superhero?"

"Nope." I scoot closer to him, letting his body heat warm me even more. "He doesn't have any powers. He's a rich guy with cool toys."

"With that logic, Iron Man isn't a superhero either."

I gasp. "You take that back. Tony Stark is a super-hero." He begins to argue, but I press a finger against his lips. "He's a scientist and managed to come back from the brink of death with his crazy smart brain. That qualifies him as a superhero."

"I think you're biased. You just like him because he's part of the *Avengers*."

"Whatever," I roll my eyes even though I know he can't see me. "You just keep believing that Batman is a superhero and leave Iron Man out of it."

"Looks like I pressed *somebody's* buttons," he mocks.

"I can always send you home," I tease. I won't send him home. I sleep better when he's here, but I'm not telling him that.

"Truce." He grabs my hand and curls his fingers around mine. "Can I go back to falling asleep?"

I pout, "I suppose."

He kisses me before closing his eyes once again. I don't bother him anymore. Instead, I watch the rest of the movie alone. Grateful for the small pockets of time I have with Derrick. It could be worse, but he's making time for me *now*, and I'll take whatever he can give.

derrick

"RHODES," Coach Wade barks from the sidelines. This is our last game before Thanksgiving, and all I've done so far this season is warm the bench. I jump at the sound of his voice since I have never heard it directed toward me during a game. "Get your ass over here. You're going to sub in for Palmer."

I don't hesitate or question him. I launch out of my chair, sending it scooting back a couple of inches, and jog to where he's standing. "Yes, sir."

Squatting next to the score table, waiting for an opportune time to switch out, I wish more than anything that Darcy was here. She does her best to come to as many home games as possible, but when we travel it's a lot harder for her. She's working at the coffee shop today, or she would have driven the three hours to watch me. And of course, the first time I actually get to play is at an away game, and she isn't here to witness it.

The crowd is deafening when I step onto the court, and it's hard for me to hear which plays my teammates are calling out. I do my best to drown them out, but it's difficult. Bentley wasn't kidding when he said it would be distracting. I didn't think much about it since my ass hasn't left my seat since the beginning of the season. I have to push past it though. My focus needs to be on the court. I really need to show Coach what I'm capable of if I want to be picked to play in the next game. Not that I have a huge amount of time to show them what I've got since there's only two minutes left in the game and were down by six points.

For those not familiar with basketball, this may not seem like a lot of time, but so much can happen within two minutes. We could gain a lead and end up winning the game, or the other team can pull further ahead and crush us. I'm going to do my best to make ensure the former happens, otherwise Coach will be pissed. We've got the ball and Bentley shoots for two. We only need five points to get ahead of our opponents, but it's going to be hard since one of our players just fouled someone.

Their point guard stands at the free-throw line, taking his first shot, and he makes it, effortlessly. The second time around, his aim is off and the ball hits the rim before Alvarado jumps up and gets the rebound. Back down by six. If we keep on like this, there's no way we're going to win.

The time on the clock ticks down, but it feels like an eternity. Thirty seconds left. Only thirty tiny seconds left to make a basket or three-pointer. I would rather win this game right now than have to go into overtime and play any longer. Not only does it make it longer that we have to stay here, but the players are worn out and tend to make pointless mistakes.

The ball is ours, and Alvarado dribbles it down the court until we are in our territory. He searches around the court, seeing who's open. I twist around the guy defending me trying to open up for shot, Alvarado passes me the ball. Seemingly out of nowhere, there's another guy from the opposing team right in front of me, waving his hands in all directions to distract me. I pivot, looking for an open shot, or somebody to pass the ball to. This guy won't get off of me, and if he keeps on he's going to end up fouling me or causing me to travel. I can't make a rookie mistake like that. I refuse to let it happen. Mind over matter, right? As I'm turning around to take the shot, regardless of the outcome, Barnes calls out my name.

I throw the ball over my head to Barnes. He's right outside the three-point line, and wide open. There isn't anyone there to get in his face or block his shot. The ball leaves his hands, and *finally* the audience quiets down waiting to see if he's going to make it or miss it. I suck in a breath, watching as the ball sails through the air, hits the backboard, and bounces on the rim twice before finally going into the basket.

The game isn't over yet. There are still four seconds

until the final buzzer, and that's just enough time for our competition to almost get the ball to half court. The person who was in my face uses all the force he can to throw the ball, hoping to make a last second shot. It doesn't get near the goal and bounces to the floor four feet from its target. We won, and it's a surreal feeling. One I didn't think I would get to experience until next semester, possibly next year.

The vastly outnumbered Hilltown fans shout their excitement from the stands. I can't wait to get back to campus and tell Darcy about it. We've won a few games, but this is the first time *I* was a part of it.

Coach calls us to the sidelines with a huge grin on his face. "Quick thinking, Rhodes." My chest puffs up at the praise. He doesn't do that with everyone, and I'm almost positive that means I'll be playing in the next game.

A hand slams down on my shoulder. Bentley turns me toward him. "Good job out there, Rhodes. Not many rookies would have passed the ball the way you did. They would have tried taking the shot even if they knew they couldn't make it." He gives my shoulder a firm squeeze before letting go. "I'm proud of you kid."

Ugh, and he ruins the sentiment with that one word. *Kid.* I'm almost twenty years old, I haven't been a kid for a while. But the compliment means a lot. This is his last year, and I want to prove that I'm capable of filling in wherever I'm needed on the team.

The team is almost running to the locker room.

Excitement and victory felt between all of us. We gather our things quickly, anxious to get on the road to Hilltown. We have a few days free from practice so we can spend time with our families over Thanksgiving. But, I just want to get back to my girl. We leave first thing in the morning for home. Tonight, is for us, though. As soon as she gets off work, we'll finally be able to spend some time together outside of basketball games and school work.

The bus pulls up in front of the gym doors and we all file out. Most of my teammates bypass the gym completely, heading straight to their cars, but I want to clean up before meeting Darcy. The guys are still rambling on about how we came back from an almost definite loss. They are usually pumped up like this after most wins, but I get to take part in that celebration today.

"Yo, Rhodes," Barnes calls out to me as he steps into the locker room. "A few of us are having a small party to celebrate our win tonight before we head home. You in?"

"Naw," I shake my head. "I'm meeting my girl in a bit." I went to my fair share of parties when I was in high school, but I don't see how these guys have time on top of school work, practice, and games go to parties.

"That's cool. If you change your mind text me." He throws his whole bag into his locker and leaves. That thing is going to smell disgusting when we get back from Thanksgiving.

Derrick: I just got back. Are you ready?

A few minutes go by before I get a response.

Darcy: One of the guys called in, so Tom asked if I could stay until eight. Can we do something after that?
Derrick: Sure thing. I'll meet you at roasted at eight.
Darcy: Can't wait to see you. And celebrate!

Word must travel fast because I didn't even tell her that we won. Or, she may have been listening to the game. Either way, I'm happy I've made her proud. Our new date time frees up a couple of hours. I can run by the party for a while before meeting Darcy. I text Barnes for the location.

Forty minutes later I walk up to what is definitely not a small party. Red cups litter the lawn and it's only 6:30. People are standing on the porch talking, or smoking, cups in their hands, and the music from inside the house is loud. Some of the window panes rattle from the force of it.

I turn to leave, wanting to make a quick escape before anyone sees me. But it's pointless. "Rhodes," Barnes yells from the porch. "Where you going? The party is this way."

Walking as slow as humanly possible I approach the house. Barnes is sitting on the railing and I have to look up to talk to him. "I was going to head out and see if Darcy is off early." I glance around at the people milling around. "I'm not sure this is my scene."

"I did tell you it was a party, didn't I?" He raises an eyebrow, no doubt thinking I'm a complete moron.

"You did." I pause for a couple of beats. "But you also said it was going to be a *small* party." I wave my hand around, gesturing to all the people standing outside without knowing how many are inside. "This definitely isn't small."

"People started showing up. That's how it is." He shrugs his shoulders as if there's no other explanation for it. "One whisper that there's a party, and all sorts of folks show up."

I shuffle back and forth. A battle being played by indecision. Do I stay for a while? Or, do I go to Roasted early? I know what I should do, but I've never been invited by teammates to anything. My role in our win tonight is most likely the only reason I'm here now.

He must see the struggle on my face. "Just stay for a little bit. Then you can go have your date night."

I can do that. I won't be shunning their invitation and I'll still get to see Darcy. "Okay, but I'm only staying for an hour tops."

* * *

Why the hell does my head hurt so bad? Slowly opening my eyes, I take in my surroundings. This isn't my room, and I'm not in my bed. As my head begins to clear, I notice the sofa I'm lying on. It's scratchy and uncomfortable. Barnes is passed out in the recliner, and few other teammates are sprawled out on any available surface.

"Oh, shit." I sit up with a start. Darcy. I never met up with her last night. I was only supposed to stay at the party for an hour. But people kept dragging me into their conversations about the game and what the rest of the season is going to look like. Those damn red cups kept showing up in my hand whenever I finished one, and I completely lost track of time. She is going to kill me.

I pat down my pockets, feeling for my phone. Pulling it out of my back pocket, I press the home button. It's dead. Of course, it is. I can't believe I've put her through this again. Not even for a good reason this time.

I knew I should have gone to Roasted instead of staying at the party. But no, I had to prove my loyalty to the team. And, for what? So, I could hurt my girl in the end? I am such an asshole. Worse, I did the one thing I know will destroy her and any chance of forgiving me.

The house is quiet, nobody is awake yet. I need to get out of here. I need to apologize. I was supposed to meet her parents tomorrow. There's no chance of that happening now.

I walk out of the house, almost sprinting to get to the dorms. What am I even going to say to her? Not that she'll listen. I wouldn't blame her either.

Instead of going to my room, I head straight to Darcy's. I knock, but there's no answer. There's no sound coming from the other side of the door, either. Where is she? Surely, she wouldn't leave without saying anything. Giving up on finding her home, I go to my own dorm room.

Travis is sitting on his bed, and he's not happy. "Dude, where the hell have you been?"

"Where's Darcy?"

"She and Cami headed home late last night. She was a complete mess." He gets in my face and pokes my chest with his finger. "Where the fuck were you?"

"I fucked up, okay." I heave a sigh. "Is that what you want to hear? The guys invited me to a party. I had time before I was supposed to meet Darcy but got caught up in basketball talk and drank too much. My phone died at some point, and I passed out there."

"I can't believe you'd be this stupid." Travis yells. "Do you not remember how long she held a grudge against you because you stood her up before?" He puts his hand up when he sees I'm about to argue. "I know last time wasn't your fault. But this time... It's all on you. Not to mention that you don't even know those guys, they could have been hazing you. But no, you want to feel like part of the team."

"I'm sorry." My shoulders sag, defeated. The high I was riding from the win last night is replaced with gut wrenching guilt and dread.

"It's not me you need to apologize to." He grabs his

suitcase. "Get cleaned up and get your shit together. We're leaving in fifteen minutes."

I plug my phone in, letting it charge while I take a shower. I do my best to scrub off the regret of last night. Regret that I stayed at the party. But mostly, regret that I let Darcy down.

My phone is lit up with notifications when I get back to the room.

Darcy: Where are you?
Darcy: Seriously, did something happen?
Darcy: You're starting to freak me out. Answer me,
please.

I hate the desperation in her text. Hate even more that I'm the one that caused it.

Darcy: I'm riding with Cami to go home. I'll see you
when I get back.

That is the nail in the coffin. There is no way she is going to forgive me this time. When it was a family emergency she felt awful for loathing me all that time. But this is different. I'm the one who screwed up. She was one of the most important things in the world to me. And I screwed it up because I wanted acceptance from my teammates.

"Let's go," Travis calls from the hallway.

I throw on the clean clothes piled in the basket at the

foot of my bed. Throwing a few more in my bag, I walk out the door, checking to make sure it's locked. Travis doesn't say anything else to me. The walk to his car is silent and will likely remain that way until we get back to Dallas. That's okay, though. I'll use the time to figure out a way to convince Darcy to give me another chance.

darcy

I DIDN'T GO HOME last night. My family would have asked questions, and I wasn't in the state of mind to answer them. Plus, we didn't get in until after midnight. Instead of driving to Dallas, I stayed the night with Cami and Tonya.

I'm beyond grateful that Tonya's parents let me stay with no questions asked. The drive here went by in a blur. I spent the entire ride trying to figure out what happened that kept Derrick from meeting me last night. Cami tried her best to keep conversation flowing, but I couldn't reciprocate.

The only thing that comes to mind is that maybe I was becoming to clingy. His late practices were starting to wear on our relationship. I wanted to see him more, and he couldn't do it. Not with practice taking over his life. As silly as it sounds, I'm almost jealous of him playing basketball. He shouldn't be with me at all times.

That's ridiculous, and I'd get tired of seeing him. But, sometimes I feel like basketball is more important than me. That I'll be put on the backburner while he strives to achieve his dreams.

"Darcy," Cami whispers next to me. "Are you awake?"

"I never really went to sleep."

"You can't do that to yourself." She wraps me into a weird sideways hug. "He fucked up, and none of that is on you."

"Why are you awake? It's early."

She sighs, "Layla woke up crying. I love that little niece of mine, but she's going to have to learn to sleep in when she's with Aunt Cami."

"She's also going to have to learn not to repeat any bad words that Aunt Cami says," Tonya's voice floats over us. When did she come in the room? Am I that zoned out to what's happening around me? I didn't even hear Layla cry.

"What?" Cami puts her hand across her chest as if she's shocked. "You don't find my colorful language useful? Not that long ago you used the same words."

"I did, but," Tonya shakes her head in frustration. "That was before I had a tiny human that could one day repeat those words. I don't want her running around her kindergarten class calling other kids assholes."

"Point taken. Though, that would be funny as hell." She ducks from the pillow Tonya throws at her.

"Remind me to not let you babysit Layla unless you have someone with you."

This is what I need right now. To be around friends that have ridiculous conversations and love each other despite their flaws. "Thank you, Tonya, for letting me crash here last night."

She waves me off. "No problem. You're welcome any time."

"Are you sure your parents are okay with that?"

"Absolutely. Cami's practically lived here our entire childhood, and now she actually does when she's not at school. They are totally fine with my friends being over. Though, I think they'll beg Cam to stay when I move out next year."

"Ugh," Cami groans. "Don't remind me. I'll probably have to find a temporary living situation for the summers when that happens." She eyes Tonya. "Unless... You and Reaf are okay with me crashing with you when I'm not at school."

Tonya ignores the comment, focusing her attention on me, while also changing Layla's diaper. How does she do that? Multitasking must be a superpower all parents receive the minute they step into the role. "Do you want to talk about it?"

As much as I hate how perceptive she is, I know I *need* to talk about what happened. Cami knows the bare bones, but I don't want this anger to fester the way it did last time. "Not really."

"But you're going to." She says matter of factly.

"Yeah, I guess." I sit up from the air mattress Cami and I slept on last night and pull my knees into my chest.

Wrapping my arms around my legs, I voice the decision I've been battling with all night. "I think I'm going to break things off with Derrick."

"As you should," Cami huffs.

"Try not to interrupt her, Cam," Tonya scolds. She really has this mother thing down. "What made you decide that?"

"Because he stood me up... Again. He didn't show up when he was supposed to and didn't answer my text messages. For all I know, he's hurt somewhere and that leaves me feeling I like a total bitch again." I glance at Layla lying on the bed with Tonya. "Sorry." She shakes her head, a silent acceptance letting me know I'm forgiven.

Cami interrupts again, "He's not." At my questioning stare she continues, "Him and Travis are on the way back to Dallas. Travis sent me a message this morning."

"Well, now I don't have to feel horrible. But, I'm curious what his excuse will be. Especially after he knows how hurt I was the last time this happened, even if it wasn't his fault then."

Cami only shrugs, not voicing her opinion. She either knows what happened, or Travis hasn't told her yet. Tonya takes this moment to ask another question. "Aside from him standing you up, are there any other reasons why you're considering breaking up with him?"

Last night isn't the only reason, but I don't want to feel stupid or like I'm weak if I tell them the rest. Cami nudges me with her elbow. "It's better if you just talk it out now. Even if I get pissed off, Tonya is the voice of reason. She'll help you figure out exactly what you should do."

I inhale, long and deep, before slowing releasing it. "There are other reasons. Mostly, I'm lonely. I know being on the team is a huge thing for him. But, I never see him. Between the practices and games, we rely on text messages most of the time." I wipe away the tear that is sliding down my cheek. "How is a new couple supposed to fight against those odds. I mean, we dated before I left for college and it was amazing. I saw him whenever I wanted, and he was always available. I feel like maybe basketball is more important to him."

"Would you ask him to throw away his dreams to be with you?" Tonya asks, quietly.

"Never," I argue. "That wouldn't be fair to him. He's worked so hard to make the team. It's the one thing he's wanted for as long as I can remember. And I support that. I go to his games when I can and watch him practice. I just thought things would be different once he made the team." I bury my face in my hands. "This is why I've never seriously dated. It's why I stick to school and work. I don't know how to do all this relationship stuff."

Tonya and Layla join us on the air mattress. She sets a couple of toys down for Layla to play with and pulls me into her arms. "Relationships are hard. I locked myself in my room when Reaf told me he loved me. It freaked me out because I couldn't figure out how I felt about him.

Well, I knew how I felt but I wasn't ready to admit it." She gives me a gentle squeeze. "All that I have to say is, you have to figure out if this relationship is worth it in the end. Can you look into the future and see him as a part of your life? If the answer is yes, then you can work this out. If not, then cut him loose now."

Can I envision a future without him? Maybe. I'm not sure. He was the first guy a fell head over heels for. Well, he's the only guy. Even when I went on dates, nobody ever piqued my interest. It's always been Derrick, whether I want to admit it or not. Now... It's time to decide if I want a future with him.

"Did I help any?" Tonya breaks into my thoughts.

"Yeah," I nod. "I definitely have a lot to think about. But, if I do try to work it out with him, I plan on making him grovel."

"Girl, I like the way you think." Tonya gets off the bed, scooping Layla up in one swift motion that causes her to giggle. "Now, let's go eat. Mom has prepared a feast, as usual."

Cami's stomach growls. "Finally, food."

I'm beyond grateful that Tonya has so seamlessly let me into their fold. We haven't talked much, but I can already tell she considers me a friend for life. I could definitely use a few of those.

The drive to my house feels like it's taking *forever*. But it's only a forty-five-minute drive. I tried telling Cami that I could get my brother to come pick me up, but she insisted on letting me use her car. Her exact words were, "I'm exactly where I want to be. If I want to go somewhere, Travis can be my chauffeur."

Who was I to argue? Besides, it gives me time to think about what Tonya said. I'd love to forgive Derrick. But at the same time, how do I know he wouldn't do it again? Being pushed to the side for other priorities sucks. I don't want to feel that pain again. Either way, I need to get my feelings under control. My family doesn't need to see me when I'm a wreck.

Cars line the driveway when I pull up, forcing me to park on the street. I've barely made it on the side when my brother, Bradley, comes running toward me. He tackle hugs me, and I almost fall down from the impact. "Little Sister, you're finally here."

"Hey," I plaster a fake smile on my face. "I made it."

"What's wrong?"

"Nothing."

He points his finger in my face, scolding me. "Don't lie to me. I know that smile. I grew up with you remember?"

"Yeah, yeah." I wave his finger away. "I don't want to talk about it right now."

"Later, then." I notice it's a statement and not a question. He fully intends on making me talk to him later. He knows me too well.

"Where is everyone?" I ask, surprised they all didn't barrel out of the house with my arrival. "I'm not feeling the love right now."

"They're inside running around like crazy people."

I scrunch up my nose. "Why?"

"Making sure they didn't forget anything when they went grocery shopping last night. But I have a feeling they'll be heading to the store in about an hour. Mom is making cheesecake and forgot to get the cream cheese."

"How do you forget the main ingredient?"

"No idea," he replies. "Whose car are you driving?"

"My friend, Cami's," I say, shrugging my shoulders. "She wouldn't take no for an answer."

"Ah, well that's cool. I guess." He turns me toward the door. "Let's go inside before Mom comes out here and makes a scene."

The house is a flurry of activity, but it stops the second I step foot into the kitchen. "Darcy, you're here." Mom envelopes me in a tight hug.

"Mom," I rasp. "I can't breathe."

"I'm sorry, Dear." She takes a small step back, giving me some space. "I'm so happy you made it." She glances behind me searching for someone. "I thought you told me you were bringing someone with you."

"I was, but there was a change in plans."

Bradley gives me a pointed stare. He knows my mood has something to do with the change. But he also looks shocked. I guess Mom didn't tell him I was bringing a guest.

"Well, that's too bad." She unties her apron and sets it on the counter. "There's plenty of food if things change."

"That's doubtful," I mutter. "So, what do you need help with?"

"Darcy, you know better than to ask to help." My grandma is sitting at the table in the connect dining room. "You're not exactly the best cook."

I roll my eyes. I burned macaroni one time, and she hasn't let me live it down. "Hi Gran." I walk to the table giving her a big squeeze. "How are you?"

She leans in and whispers, "I'd be doing a lot better if your mom would break out the wine already."

Laughing, I sneak to the small refrigerator that holds the wine. There's an open bottle on the first rack, and I pour some in a glass. "Here you go, Gran. But if she asks, I didn't do it."

My aunts, uncles, and cousins won't be here until tomorrow, but the house if full of noise. It's nice being back home, and what I need right now. I poke around the living room, looking for the board games. Finally finding the one I'm looking for I walk back into the dining room.

"Anyone want to play Scrabble with me?" I begin laying the game out, hoping someone will want to join me.

"Do I look like I want to get my ass kicked?" My brother asks from opposite me.

"Bradley, language." My mother throws a dishrag at him.

He ducks, but it lands on the other side of the table, nowhere near us. "Sorry, Mom." He turns his attention back to me. "Why can't we play Monopoly or something?"

"Because," I argue. "It takes forever and you always cheat."

His lack of defense lets me know that I'm right. He's cheated at that game since we were kids. He thinks I don't know that he hides the monopoly money in the bathroom and gets it under the guise of going to the restroom. Since I figured it out, I've refused to play with him. There's no point if I'm going to lose.

"Fine," he relents. "I'll play with you. It's not like I have anything better to do."

I snort. "Obviously. You definitely don't have a girl-friend to take up all your time."

"You don't have anyone either."

I flinch. I know he didn't mean anything by it because I never said anything to him about Derrick. But the jab hurts all the same. "Whatever, let's play."

We're halfway into the game, and of course I'm winning, when there's a knock at the door. It's definitely not someone we're expecting because our family just walks in like they live there. "Mom, can you get that? I don't want to leave my pieces because Bradley will look at them."

"Yes," she sighs, familiar with the routine because she knows it's true. He'll take any opportunity he can to beat me.

A few seconds later she comes back into the kitchen. "Darcy, there's a young man at the front door for you."

No, this can't be happening. There's no way that Derrick showed up here. I scoot back from the chair, hoping it's Travis. There's no reason for him to be here, but anything would be better than Derrick.

As I walk into the entryway, I hear Bradley's chair screech across the floor. Ugh, big brothers. They always have to be nosey. I come to a stop when I see Derrick standing in the doorway. He looks like he hasn't slept in days, and his hair is a mess. He's obviously been running his fingers through it.

"Who the hell are you?" I hear Bradley bellow from right behind me. This isn't going to go well.

derrick

"UH, HI," I wave awkwardly. This must be her brother, and he's glaring at me like I'm a threat to his baby sister. Maybe I am. "I'm Derrick, Darcy's, um, friend."

It kills me saying friend, but right now I don't know if I'm even that. The pain that flickers across her face is like a punch to the gut. I'm definitely in deep shit.

"Friend?" He scoffs. "Why haven't I heard of you before?"

Not going to lie, that stings. Has she not told her family about me? Is she ashamed?

"Bradley," Darcy cuts in. "Go away. This isn't any of your business."

"Is *he* why you were upset when you got here?"

She doesn't answer him. Knowing that she came home still upset sends another wave of guilt through me, as if I haven't felt enough. Her arms are crossed tightly over her chest, and her eyes are glistening. Shit, she's about to cry and it's all my fault.

"Dar, can we talk?" I ask, hoping she'll say yes. I'll beg if I have to. I can't lose her because of my mistake. I'll do anything to ensure that she's mine.

"Hell no, you can't talk to her." Her brother booms.

"Bradley," the woman, I'm assuming Darcy's mom, calls from just out of sight. "Get in here, now."

He bristles, but eventually turns around and leaves the room. As he enters the other room, he looks at me one final time with a hard stare. Message received, buddy. I won't hurt your sister. At least, not anymore than I already have.

"Dar?"

"Yeah," she pauses. "Just... Let me grab a jacket."

She returns a few moments later wearing a Hilltown U hoodie. Her face is set in determination. Whether it's to hear me out, or let me go, I don't know. But it sends a spike of fear through me.

I start for the bench that sits on her front porch but she grabs my arm. "Let's take a walk." It's a statement that brooks no argument. Nope, this isn't good at all.

We walk a few minutes in gut wrenching silence. What's going on inside her head? I can't fathom that it's anything good. Otherwise she would have something by now.

"I'm so-" I begin, but she cuts me off.

"What the hell are you doing here, Derrick?" She stops abruptly. "I told you I would talk to you when we got back from Thanksgiving break. What made you think it was a good idea to just show up at my house?"

"I don't know. I needed to see you and tell you how sorry I am that I screwed up." She's not going to listen to me, and I'm ninety percent sure I've blown my chances with her.

She throws her hands up in the air, exasperated. "And showing up at my parents' house was what you came up with? You could have sent me a text or call."

"Like you would have answered. Your last text made it pretty clear that you didn't want to talk to me."

"And yet, here you are." Darcy sighs and shakes her head, clearly frustrated with me. At the same time, my heart breaks at the thought of having to give her up. I shouldn't have come, but I thought if I made the first move *maybe* she would forgive me.

Her arms are wrapped around her middle. I'm not sure if it's because she's cold or because I'm here, and I don't want to cause her any more stress. "I'm sorry. I'll leave." I turn, walking in the direction we came from. "I hope you have a good Thanksgiving with your family."

I'm approximately five feet from where I left her when I feel a hand clasp around mine. We stay like that, in this weird sort of silent limbo. The only thing that can be heard is the gentle rustle of leaves from the light breeze.

Finally, she speaks. "Don't go. We do need to talk, and what better time than now since you're here."

I swivel around to face her with a tight smile. "If it

makes you feel any better, Travis told me I should wait and give you time." She lets loose a soft laugh, and that gives me hope. "Obviously... I didn't listen."

She snorts, "Obviously." She takes a few deep breaths before jumping headfirst into this conversation. "So, what happened last night? Where were you?"

There's no good answer for that, and she's going to think I'm a moron for my reasoning. "Well," I stutter. "I was at a party with some of my teammates."

Her eyes widen, then her eyebrows scrunch together into two little angry arches. "You blew me off for a freaking party?"

"No," I blurt. "It wasn't like that. I turned the party invitation down at first, but then you texted me telling me you had to work late. I figured I would go for an hour and then meet you at the coffee shop." I take a step closer to her willing her to understand. "I lost track of time and they kept giving me drinks. Then my phone died and I passed out on the couch. "

"That doesn't make it okay," she whispers, hurt by my confession. "I just don't understand why you would choose a party over me. Especially when we've had so little time together."

"I know it must seem like that, but I promise you that wasn't my intention. I just wanted to feel accepted by my team. I didn't mean to stay all night, and I didn't mean to stand you up."

There's a bench lining the sidewalk a few feet away and she walks us toward it. Apparently, she has to sit down for us to have this conversation and I don't blame her at all. This whole situation I put us in sucks. "Why do you feel like you need to be accepted by them? You're an amazing basketball player. Your coach sees it, and he put you in the game at a crucial moment in the game yesterday. Bentley saw something in you, otherwise he wouldn't have wasted the time to practice with you. The opinions of your other teammates shouldn't matter."

Sitting in silence, I take in everything she said. She's right, I know she is. But I had this idea of how things would be if I made the team and the close friendships I had hoped to have. "I know that. But these guys never talked to me after the games, I didn't exist to them. But when I was invited to the party, it felt like maybe I could have the camaraderie I had with my high school team. The sad thing is, I told Barnes I needed to leave in an hour, and he didn't have my back. I'm not sure I want a friendship with someone like that."

"Kind of like how I feel," she mutters under her breath.

"What?" I ask, wanting to make sure that I heard her correctly.

She sighs, "I said, kind of like how I feel."

"What does that mean?" It comes out defensive. I don't want for it to be, but a worrisome feeling inside of me says that it has something to do with me.

"It's going to sound dumb." She pulls her hand from mine and shoves them into the pocket of her hoodie.

"What I said sounded ridiculous, but you heard me

out." Placing my now vacant hand on her knee, I rub tiny circles into the rough denim. Coaxing her to open up to me. "Let me do the same for you."

"I'm not trying to sound like a needy person, but there are so many times I felt like basketball and the team were more important than me. I always do my best to make time for you, even when I work late. But the same wasn't reciprocated. I know your worn out after practice, but sometimes text messages and phone calls aren't enough. We're practically across the quad from each other, but only see each other once a week."

I didn't mean to make her feel like that. Like basketball is more important, but I can see where she's coming from. Especially after my massive fuck up last night.

"I'm sorry I made you feel that way. But know that *nothing* is more important than you. Not even basketball." I slide off the bench so I can look her in the eyes. Her focus on the ground, ashamed of her admission. "What can I do to make it up to you? I'll do anything. And, I promise to do my best to ensure you know how much you mean to me. I'll even quit the team if I have to."

She sucks in a breath. "Absolutely not. You are going to stay on that team. You've worked so hard to make it, and I will not allow you to throw it away." She stands so quickly that I nearly fall backward. "But, I need time to think. Just a couple of days. I don't want to move on with you and sweep this under the rug like it doesn't matter. Last night sucked."

I stand slowly. "I understand."

Gently stroking my arm, she continues. "I'm not saying it's over between us. What we've said today is a step in the right direction. I need to be sure about a few things before I put my heart on the line again."

Leaning in on her tiptoes she places a soft kiss on my cheek and walks away. I can give her time. I don't want to, but I'll do it for her. I want her to be certain she can rely on me to hold her heart.

Hilltown is quiet today. I suspect most people won't come back until tomorrow. My car had been sitting in the garage since I came here at the beginning of the semester, so I drove it down here a day early. I needed some time away from my family and Travis to process everything with Darcy.

I've been thinking over how she said I made her feel, and I can see where she's coming from. My life lately has been all basketball all the time. Even my grades are starting to slip. And that's one thing I can't let happen. If I start to fail I can't play ball and my parents will be pissed. I need to do a complete overhaul on how I manage my time, and make sure I put priorities first.

Now, to figure out what I can do to make sure Darcy doesn't push me away. Obviously, I can't wow her with my outdoor skills. It's not my strong point and it's cold at night. Maybe I'll rethink that. It's more reason to snuggle close. She likes comics and stuff like that. Maybe that will show her that I can be supportive of her interests the way she is mine. Pulling out my phone, I search for nearby comic stores, and see what movies are playing. I'm going to spoil her if she'll allow me. I just need the chance to talk to her.

darcy

"I DON'T UNDERSTAND why you're going over there to talk to him," Cami complains. We got to our dorm about an hour ago, and she's not happy about the decision I've come to. But she'll support me. She'll also be the one helping to put me back together if this all blows up in my face.

"You know why. We talked about it the entire way home."

"Well, I'll be here either way. I just hope he realizes the olive branch you're handing him."

I put up the last of my clothes. "We'll never know if I don't get out of here."

"I'll see you later. Good luck."

"Thanks, I'll need it," I mutter as I walk out of our room. Not because I'm worried about how he'll take what I have to say, but because I'm worried I'll get tongue tied and it will come out wrong. I'll be vulnerable and more like my former self than I've been in a long time.

The walk to Derrick's building is cold. The temperature is dropping day by day announcing Winter's arrival. I pull the pink and black knit hat down over my ears in a pointless effort to keep them warm. The oncoming of Winter always saddens me. Everything dies, and the world looks duller. It's hard to be in good mood when that happens. It's also making me second guess showing up Derrick's unannounced. I'm already at the front door to his building so there's no going back.

The elevator takes forever to get to the lobby, and I'm about to take the stairs when the doors finally slide open. Travis is walking out of them.

"I guess Cami gave you a heads up that I was on my way over."

He nods. "I was beginning to wonder if you were going to chicken out."

"Nope. I'm going up there to talk to him. We'll see what happens after that."

I walk into the elevator, but Travis puts his hand out to keep the doors from closing. "He does love you. He has for a while now. He's just not used to having to own up to his screw ups. I think your talk will go better than you expect."

"Thanks." The doors finally close. I press the button for their floor and wait as the elevator takes me up. I think I already knew that he loved me. Nothing in particular, but a gut feeling. I've felt the same way about him, too. It's time to lay it all out on the line.

Knocking on his door is surreal. It's usually him showing up unannounced at my place. I wonder how he'll like it when the tables are turned. It takes forever for him to answer. "Dude, why are you knocking? You liv-"

The words die on his tongue the second he realizes it's not Travis. "Hi, Derrick."

"Darcy, what are you doing here?" His eyes are wide, and I think he may be in shock. He definitely wasn't expecting me to show up at his room any time soon.

"Can we talk?"

"Yeah, come in." Pushing books off his bed, he makes a space for me to sit down. He rolls the chair out from under the desk, before taking a seat. "Are you thirsty? Do you want something to drink?"

"No, I'm good," I laugh. It's adorable how nervous he is.

He nods. After a few seconds he says, "I'm so sorry, Darcy. I'll make it up to you however you want me to."

"It's okay." His head snaps back, confused by what I just said. "I did a lot of thinking over the weekend. And I don't want this to be the end for us, but things have to change. I know our lives are busy, but we still need to make time for each other."

"I completely agree." He stares at me, blinking. He can't believe I'm here, and I feel a rush of satisfaction that I was able to surprise him. "What made you decide to give us another shot?"

"When Cami and I left Tuesday night, she didn't take me home. We stayed with Tonya. That girl is a wealth of information. Anyway, she asked me if I could see a future without you." I let that sink in for him before I continue. "I can, but it would suck. You make me happy, and accept me. Weird tendencies and all."

"I've told you to embrace your weird for as long as I can remember. Your weirdness is one of the things I love about you." His eyes go wide with the slip of the "L" word.

"So, you do love me?"

"I have since that summer. You're the only person I've thought about since then. And, even when you were being mean as hell to me when I came to visit Travis, I reveled in it because it meant you had some sort of feeling for me."

I roll my eyes. "Now, who's the weird one?"

He scoots his chair closer to the bed. Closer to me. "I'll be weird with you."

"I love you, Weirdo." I throw my arms around him and pull him to me before kissing him like my life depends on it. Even with all the ups, downs, and adjustments I know will come, I can't actually imagine a world without him by my side.

CHRISTMAS BREAK MIGHT BE my favorite time of the school year. We're out for a month before having to go back to the hustle and bustle of balancing studying and anything else we are involved in.

It's been a few weeks since Darcy showed up at my dorm room and decided that she still wanted me in her life. We made it a priority to see each other more. She even helped me set up a calendar for everything I'm involved in. It helped with managing what I needed to do and what I wanted to do. Which was spend time with her any chance I could. I'd even sit at Roasted and do my homework if it meant I was able to see her.

I considered confronting Barnes about being a shitty friend. But honestly, it wasn't worth the wasted breath. He's one of those that is never going to change. He thinks he's hot shit just because he's on the team. He's a first-year player like me, but I'm not willing to do anything to screw up my future on the team or with Darcy.

Right now, we're gathered around a firepit at Tonya's house. I finally met her tonight, and I get what Cami said about her being a smart person. She thinks before she speaks and doesn't dole out advice unless she would take it.

Darcy is sitting in my lap under the pretense of body warmth. Honestly, I think she's just happy to spend time with me away from the constraints of school and work. The December night air is bitter cold, but Tonya and Reaf wanted a place for all of us to hang out without waking up Layla. I applaud Tonya for being such an awesome mom at a young age. And for being able to be friends with her ex and his girlfriend. It's not often you see that. I wouldn't have believed it's possible if I didn't see it with my own eyes.

Cami and Travis are sitting next to us in the hammock, softly swaying. "Where's Marshall?" Cami asks Jake who's sitting across from us.

He shrugs his shoulders. "I don't know. When I talked to him earlier he said something about not wanting to be around all the couples. I think he's frustrated because he doesn't know if he should contact Bianca or not."

"That's your friend, right?" Cami points the question toward Jake's girlfriend, Charleigh.

"Yep. She's been a mess since he left, but she's

getting better every day. I'm not sure what would happen if she saw him again."

Darcy shivers when a gust of wind hits us. "Do you want to go home?"

She shakes her head. "I'm good. Besides, I think Tonya wants us to help with wedding planning while we're here."

"Speaking of," Tonya stands up. "Why don't we grab some hot chocolate, put on some *Buffy*, and knock this to-do list out."

The girls all stand up, and I swear I hear Charleigh mutter something about the weird obsession with that show. I watch Darcy file in with them, happy that she has a group of people that accept her for who she is. Just like I have.

I look at each of the guys watching their respective girls walk inside. They have us wrapped around their fingers, and they know it. I'm sure each of us would do whatever they wanted no questions asked.

"Aren't you going to be included in the planning?" I ask Reaf.

"Nope. I'm good with whatever makes her happy."

We are putty in their hands. But I'll be whatever Darcy needs me to be. That night my gramps died tore us apart, but another night brought us closer together. I wouldn't change the past year and half if I could. We're closer than we've ever been, and I know wherever she goes I'll follow.

* * *

Prologue

Going back to school is the last thing I want to do. It means leaving her, the one person I feel a connection with. I didn't see her coming, and she's my polar opposite in every way. But I can't stay, and I can't ask her to leave.

The tattoo shop, Life in Ink, is slow for the time of day. Usually when the sun starts to go down people make their way into this part of town, hoping to get a tattoo from Charleigh or Bianca. The guys do amazing work, too. But the girls...They are what draw the crowd in. Charleigh's marketing efforts have definitely helped in that area.

Sophie is at the desk in the lobby, checking her phone while trying not to stare at Adrian. When is he going to realize that she has it bad for him? It's apparent to anyone who has been in their presence for more than five minutes. "Hey, Soph. Is Bianca around?"

She's so startled she almost falls out her chair. "Oh, hi Marshall. Um," she glances around the shop. Not really looking for anybody in particular but doing her best to keep from making eye contact with me. "She called in today."

"Is she okay?" She hasn't responded to my text messages or answered the phone. That's not out of the ordinary since she's not a fan of having it on her all the time. But knowing she called in doesn't sit well with me.

"I don't know," she shrugs. "She only said that she wasn't feeling well."

"Okay." She never calls in to work. Tattooing people is her entire world and her passion. I know for a fact she had a few appointments today, and she's not one to let them down or reschedule. Something weird is going on. "Can you tell her to call me if you hear from her?"

Sophie only nods. Relieved, she turns back to her phone. I turn to the front door to leave when I spot Charleigh coming out of her studio. Her eyes go wide. Something is definitely up.

"Charleigh, have you heard from Bianca?" She backpedals, rushing to get out of my line of sight. It's no use, I follow her into the room. "Why do you look so panicked? You've talked to her, haven't you?"

She sighs. "Yes, I've talked to her."

"She's not sick, is she?"

Shaking her head, she fiddles with a sketchbook sitting on the counter. "She's not. She doesn't want to see you today."

"Why not?" I demand. It's my last chance to see her before I leave this evening. I wanted to take her to lunch and make it special for us.

"She said it would be too hard for her." Charleigh picks up a pen and begins to sketch, keeping herself busy while delivering news she knows is going to destroy me. "She fell for you over the summer. Hook, line, and sinker.

Seeing you leave will only tear her apart knowing she can't go with you. And you aren't staying."

"How am I supposed to tell her goodbye?" I sit in her tattoo chair and bury my face in my hands. I fell for her, too. It wasn't supposed to happen. I was just looking to spend time with someone I found interesting. Instead… I found a person I would fight for. But I have to leave. I've already registered for my classes. And, even though my parents aren't struggling, I can't let them take the financial hit that dropping my classes would entail.

"I don't know, Marsh. But don't blow up her phone. It's difficult enough for her already."

Sighing, I get to my feet. "Thanks. Will you tell her I'll miss her and that I'll be back in December."

"Yeah, I'll tell her. But give her time to heal. She doesn't get close to anyone, and frankly I'm a little surprised she let you in."

"Thank you." I give her a quick hug. She's become a part of our group since she started dating Jake. More than that, she's good for him. "You better send me pictures of Layla. Just in case Jake forgets." Layla is Jake's seven-month old baby, and I'm happy he got his shit together so he could be a part of her life.

"I will." She looks me over, seeing the sadness all over my face. "Things will work out the way they are supposed to. Like I said give her time, but don't give up hope." She winks, and I let myself believe her if only until I walk out of this shop.

With a wave and quick look at Bianca's area, I leave

Life in Ink. Regret passing over me and wishing I had more time with the girl that took me by surprise.

Pick up your copy of *My Only Wish is You*!

acknowledgments

This is the part where I get all sentimental about the people that have helped me while writing this book. I couldn't do this without my tribe, and I'm so freaking happy to have each and every one of you in my life.

Nessa, you're my girl. I couldn't do life without you. I'm so glad we became best friends. You are my rock when I need someone to lean on, and the person who kicks my ass when I need to get in gear. I love you, girl.

My sprinting group: Kelsie, Tasha, and Ashley, you made my nights entertaining. I will never look at a guy with chest hair the same way again. Thanks for distracting me and cheering me on. I'm beyond lucky to have found y'all!

My Alpha Squad. You all are amazing. Whether it's coming up with titles or fixing my five million typing errors, you have been an amazing help with this story. I'm so happy that you all believe in me and love my characters as much as I do. Jennifer, Cass, Cindy, Kristin, Carine, Melanie, and Mistee, I don't know what I would do without you.

Shelly and Victoria, thank you for all the hard work you do to help me with each release. You both make my life a million times easier. Jess, thank you for the encouraging words, and making me want to exceed my expectations.

Mom and Dad, thank you for letting me bore you with my book talk. I know I go overboard sometimes but I'm grateful to have the both of you in my corner.

Hubs, Boy Child, and Wee One... I love you all. The three of you are why I chase my dreams and constantly try to better myself. My life would be incomplete without you. Go after your dreams, fulfill them, and go after more. Also, thank you for picking up the slack while I was writing this book.

Readers and bloggers, thank you for picking up my book. It means the world to me that my words, and characters, have made their way into your hearts. I wouldn't be able to do this whole author gig if it wasn't for you.

also by katrina marie

The Taking Chances Series

Welcome to Your Life

Cruel and Beautiful World

Ways to Go

Remember That Night

My Only Wish is You

From This Moment

Shoot Down the Stars

Love Will Save Your Soul

Gone in Love Series

Out of the Ashes Series

Cocky Hero Club

Big Baller

Silverwood Bulldog Series

Baseball & Broadway

Katrina Marie lives in the Dallas area with her husband, two children, and fur baby. She is a lover of all things geeky and Gryffindor for life. When she's not writing you can find her at her children's sporting events, or curled up reading a book.

Visit her online: katrinamarieauthor.com

Sign up for my newsletter for extras from Welcome to Your Life: http://bit.ly/2BlDSsZ

facebook.com/KatrinaMarieAuthor

twitter.com/katrmarieauthor

instagram.com/katrinamarieauthor

amazon.com/Katrina-Marie/e/B0749SZVTK/ref=dp_byline_cont_ebooks_1

bookbub.com/profile/katrina-marie

pinterest.com/katrinamarieauthor

www.ingramcontent.com/pod-product-compliance
Lightning Source LLC
Chambersburg PA
CBHW061810190726
48289CB00007B/2141